Lydia Cassett reading the morning paper:
 a novel

Lydia Cassatt Reading the Morning Paper

Lydia Cassatt
Reading
the Morning Paper

a novel by

Harriet Scott Chessman

a copublication of The Permanent Press
and Seven Stories Press

NEW YORK • LONDON • TORONTO • SYDNEY

For inquiries related to English-language distribution and North American rights contact:

Seven Stories Press
140 WATTS STREET, NEW YORK, NY 10013
info@sevenstories.com

For editorial inquiries, or matters related to foreign-language rights or film rights, contact:

The Permament Press
4170 NOYAC ROAD, SAG HARBOR, NY 11963
shepard@thepermanentpress.com

In Canada:
HUSHION HOUSE, 36 NORTHLINE ROAD, TORONTO, ONTARIO M4B 3E2

In the U.K.:
TURNAROUND PUBLISHER SERVICES LTD., UNIT 3, OLYMPIA TRADING ESTATE
COBURG ROAD, WOOD GREEN, LONDON N22 6TZ

In Australia:
TOWER BOOKS, 9/19 RODBOROUGH ROAD, FRENCHS FOREST NSW 2086

Library of Congress Cataloging-in-Publication Data

Chessman, Harriet Scott.
Lydia Cassatt reading the morning paper / Harriet Scott Chessman.
—A Permanent press/Seven Stories Press 1st ed.
p.   cm.
ISBN 1-58322-272-3
1. Cassatt, Lydia, d. 1882—Fiction. 2. Bright's disease—Patients—Fiction.
3. Cassatt, Mary, 1844–1926—Fiction. 4. Artists' models—Fiction.
5. Women painters—Fiction. 6. Sisters—Fiction. I. Title.
PS3553.H4225 L93 2001b
813'.54—dc21   2001032111

9 8 7 6 5 4 3

College professors may order examination copies
of Seven Stories Press titles for a free six-month trial period. To order, visit
www.sevenstories.com/textbook, or fax on school letterhead to (212) 226-1411.

Book design by POLLEN/Stewart Cauley and India Amos

Printed in the U.S.A.

The imperfect is our paradise.

—Wallace Stevens, "The Poems of Our Climate"

This story is based on the lives of the American Impressionist painter Mary Cassatt (1844–1926) and her sister Lydia Cassatt (1837–1882). Each of the five chapters centers around one of Mary's paintings of Lydia. I have attempted to be as accurate as possible about the Cassatts' lives, yet this is most definitely a work of fiction. The paintings themselves, so moving and appealing, have drawn me to the figure of Lydia, painted again and again by her sister. I have thought, imagined, and dreamt my way into her world.

CHAPTERS

Woman Reading

In my dream, I walk down the five flights of stairs to the avenue in Paris, yet when I open the heavy front door, I am on the porch at Hardwicke. Robbie is pulling May in a wagon on the pebbled drive, and out in the meadow, I know, Aleck is already beginning to urge his horse over the jumps. The day is bright, and I run toward the barn to saddle up Juno, when suddenly

i.

"Could you model for me tomorrow, Lyd?"

May's looking at me with a kind of urgency and hopefulness. I've been showing her some new dress patterns, as we linger at the table after breakfast. She looks sweet for a moment, and worried, and I say, "I think so."

"Mother thinks it will make you too tired."

"Yes, I do," calls Mother, from her room.

"*N'importe quoi.* I'm so much better now."

I drink my coffee, picturing the walk to May's studio. It's only a few streets away, just off the place Pigalle, but I haven't been well, and in any case I've become attached to this perch, our apartment on avenue Trudaine, in the *9ème arrondissement*. We're in Paris, and yet we're also in our own world, five stories up; we've become a bit like a nation, The Cassatt Nation, small and besieged, at times, and independent. In the kitchen, the new maid Lise is clattering the

5

dishes. Father rustles the paper in the parlor; he's been reading us bits out of *Le Petit Parisien*.

I rise to look out the window. Over the tops of the apartments across from us, I see the white and cream buildings scrambling up the hill of Montmartre, among trees and gardens. Looking down to the avenue Trudaine, I see a girl in a royal blue coat and a red hat race along the street with a dog. I'm in love with all of this, this bright and foreign life.

"I could have the carriage brought round, Lyddy."

"Such a short distance, May! Don't be silly!"

"The carriage is a good idea," Mother says, coming into the dining room. She's wearing her specs and her old white morning gown, with her light wool shawl. How old she's begun to look, I think.

I know May needs me to model. It's partly the cost, of course, to hire someone else. To pay a model—well, it adds up, and Father's at her constantly now about making her way, and covering all of her own expenses, for the studio too. "Think for yourself, May," he said this morning, as we sat down to breakfast, "think what this costs us, and tally up your sales this year. Got to consider this."

I glimpse two young men on the avenue, elegantly dressed, talking and gesturing energetically as they stroll. I open the long window and lean over the small *balcon* for a moment, to catch a better look.

Perhaps May knows them? Maybe they're on their way to one of the cafés at the place Pigalle, to smoke cigarettes, and drink coffee, and argue about art. I see such men, often, sitting outside a café like Degas' favorite, Le Rat Mort. Women too go there; sometimes, as I walk with May, I see mothers and grandmothers sitting happily, with pretty children, eating sliced melon or apricot pie.

Once I saw a woman sitting close to a young man. I glimpsed him nuzzling her, kissing her neck, and, before I could look away, I caught the expression on her face, a mixture of coolness and knowledge and pleasure.

"I think I'll go to the Bois today, give your horse some exercise," Father says cheerfully to May.

I look over May's shoulder. She's studying a pattern I chose at Worth's, for an evening gown with an off-the-shoulder *décolleté*.

"It would look delicious on you, in a yellow silk," I say.

May looks up. I can see she's studying me with her painter's eyes. Inwardly, I flinch; I feel shy, always, when someone looks at me. She's my younger sister, by a full seven years, I remind myself, even if she's thirty-four now, and yet I feel so much younger than May sometimes. I can't help wondering what she sees. I'm as plain as a loaf of bread.

As if divining my thoughts, May smiles. She peels an orange with a little knife. "You can look away. You can be reading this time."

"Ah, yes." I smile as I sit down across the table from her. May knows me well, for within this Cassatt Nation, my own small acre has treasures of books stashed everywhere, in the elbows of trees, beneath berry bushes, on benches by streams. My little house is composed of books: English and French novels, and books of poetry too, gold-edged. I, who am moderate in so much, who bend myself to family life, am most immoderate once I'm in my acre. I read for hours, with passion, ardently wishing the stone wall around me to hold, the little gate to feel the pressure of no hand, the latch to grow rusty.

"I wish we had brought more of that honey back to Paris from the country," Mother says, her specs slipping down her nose. She's writing a list for Lise's shopping today.

"I'm sure we can find good honey somewhere in Paris," May says drily. "You didn't have any orange this morning, Lyddy, did you?" she asks, holding out a section of hers. The peelings make a sphere on her plate.

I accept the orange sliver.

"Maybe you can just do the back of my head," I suggest.

"*Mais non*, Lyddy. I want your lovely face."

She looks at me teasingly, and *for a moment I am riding in the country again, in West Chester, Pennsylvania. It's early spring, snow still on the ground in places, and we must have been back from our long stay in Europe for a year or so. We had buried Robbie in Germany. I picture myself riding with Aleck and his friend from Yale, Thomas Houghton. The day is chilly, and, once we've dismounted, I take off my gloves and rub my hands together, holding them to my mouth. Thomas is close to me. "Cold?" he asks, catching my hands in his, chafing, bringing them halfway to his mouth.*

"How about a profile?" May asks.

"If it helps you out, May, yes."

"You're helping me immensely. We'll begin tomorrow morning."

I think of the quiet day tomorrow would have been, West Chester swirled away into the past now, along with Philadelphia and Pittsburgh, my life a new one here in Paris, talking to Mother and Father, reading a novel, looking through my patterns, hoping through it all to make some miraculous leap out of my condition, to become healthy again. I contemplate the slow descent down five flights to the avenue, and the slow walk by May's side, through a late September morning. I prefer the longer journey, along avenue Trudaine to the park at the place d'Anvers, because of the trees, the green island. Then up we walk to the busy boulevard de Rochechouart and the boulevard de Clichy, coming at last to the place Pigalle, my body increasingly assaulted and aroused by a myriad of things: the trolleys, the laborers, the shop assistants, the

9

pavements in front of cafés still damp from being washed, the scent of coffee and bread, and of manure too.

"Tomorrow morning, yes," I say, feeling worried but brave, and picturing my little boat, leaks and all, bobbing along in the wake of my sister's grander vessel, sailing to Heaven knows where.

ii.

I sink into the plump green chair in May's studio, holding the paper.

After breakfast this morning, Mother asked me a dozen times if I really felt well enough, demanding that May paint only for an hour, or at most two. As I put on my bonnet and gloves, Father too began to fret. "Are you warm, Lyddy?" he asked. "Make sure she stands up to stretch, at least every half-hour, May." Then he called to Lise to "bring Mademoiselle Cassatt's slippers, and—what about a small pillow?" After all this fuss, as always, I questioned the entire idea of modeling. If I became exhausted before I arrived at the door of our apartment, how could I possibly think of helping May?

I listen to the city's constant clatter and clamor outside the windows of May's studio, and I think of the shops we passed this morning, so much more seductive, even in this gritty district, than those I remember in the States. Each shop window lures me with something delicious or fine: *prâlines*, cut flowers, linens and silks. "It makes America look pretty bare, doesn't it?" May said to me last week, and she's right, in a sense. Certainly shops like the ones near the new Opéra and the Tuileries amaze the wealthiest of our American friends. All of them flock to the Bon Marché too, and the other *grands magasins*, filled, layer after layer, like the inside of wedding cakes, with things to buy. Philadelphia can't compare, and yet I sometimes miss those modest shops. Something appeals to me in restraint.

Le Petit Journal becomes absurdly heavy in my hands, and my arms ache. I've read all the articles, and editorial opinions, and advertisements too, and now I'm wishing I had my book. "Women are always pictured reading books," May said, as we set up this morning. "A newspaper is perfect. And what could be better than *Le Petit Journal*? It's so modern. It shows you're a thinking woman." I yearn, though, for the novel I began yesterday and left sitting on my bed—*Madame Bovary*. I'm reading it for the second time, and I relish it even more now than I did when I was younger.

As I pose, I remember how Mother loved sitting for her portrait last spring. She would make light of her contribution—"All I do is lounge in a soft chair and read the paper," she'd say, waving her hand—but she would seem happier than usual, as if she had been granted a second life in the studio, more carefree, more glamorous, than this one. Father's irritations and demands seemed to reach her only through a haze. "Yes, my dear," she would say happily, "I'll be sure to come home tomorrow well in time for lunch," or "Of course I'll write to Aleck and to Gardner tomorrow."

When I first saw Mother's picture, the painting seemed reckless, May's brushstrokes bold, Mother's *déshabillé* a harum-scarum wash of colors. I felt wonder, and jealousy too. This shimmer, this feeling—how under Heaven had she created this? The painting showed Mother, simply herself, with her specs, reading the paper as on any ordinary morning. Yet May had caught a feeling, a whole moment, in paint. It was every bit as striking as Berthe Morisot's pictures, and more appealing to me than any of the ones I'd seen by May's other new friends, even Renoir.

How courageous May had become! To paint the ordinary,

a woman in her morning dress reading *Le Figaro*, and to make the picture dance like this, to feel unbound by all the things one had been taught, or by the paintings put up each spring at the Salon, so dark and classical. Mother praised May's painting in her offhand manner—"Lovely light, don't you think, Lyddy, and look how May used the mirror!"—but I knew she felt proud.

iv.

Around the rectangle of *Le Petit Journal*, the parquet floors of May's studio shine. I can see the edge of one of her Turkish rugs, the rose and gray one, in intricate patterns. My arms and shoulders feel sore.

"A cup of tea, Lyddy?"

"Thanks, yes."

"I've made you pose for over an hour. Mother would be furious."

As I put the newspaper down, tiny pinpricks run into my fingers. The little gold hands on the clock above the mantel say half past ten.

May moves about the studio with her usual quickness. She darts, like a bird. She's slender, almost too thin, really. As she opens the tin of tea, I think of Mother, when she was younger and healthier, making tea for us on Sundays, wherever we lived, and I picture May too, as a little girl on a pony, her face stubborn and shining. *"Let me try,"* she's saying to Aleck and me, as Robbie looks on from the gate. She's four or so, and I must be about eleven, Aleck nine, and how old would Robbie be? Seven? We're in the meadow by our country house, Hardwicke, before our move to Philadelphia. Aleck and I love to jump our horses, small jumps. The meadow at Hardwicke's just been mown, and the ground is uneven. Robbie swings on the gate, and *"Let me try," she says again. "You're too little," Aleck says, but in a moment she's in the air, her small figure rising inches above her pony's back, and soon she's jumping, again, and again, and Aleck shouts, "Good jumping, Mame!" and I shout, "Careful!" I'm angry with her, because she never listens. At dinner that night, when I begin to tell the story, May and Robbie interrupt, and then Father says she should have lessons with us if she's so bent on jumping.*

As May brings me my tea, she reminds me of a mermaid; something about her floats, skims the waves. For a moment I wonder what it would be like to be an artist. How does a woman make such a choice? Or is it something that comes to one, like a gift from heaven?

"Et bien, you look thoughtful, Lyd."

I smile, brushing the air in front of my nose as if to say, It's nothing. Sipping my tea, walking about May's studio, I study some of her pictures: a woman holding out a treat for a dog, a woman reading, sketches of Mother by the lamp at home. I come upon one of May's self-portraits too, the little gouache on paper, and think how much more striking it is than some of the other pictures, and how odd she looks in it, not quite like herself. She appears serious and jaunty, leaning hard into a green cushion. Her dress is lovely, the white one Madame Ange made for her, but her face looks sad, and stubborn too.

Bold she is, and not like other women.

"Do you like this one?" May is at my shoulder.

"I do. Well, 'like' may not be the right word."

"No?"

"I find it formidable."

"Well, I don't mind being formidable!" May slips her arm through mine.

"Yes, and I admire the dress too."

"You helped me find the material for that dress, Lyddy, *tu te souviens?*"

It occurs to me that May has in this self-portrait an air of someone looked at—looked at by someone else, I mean, and not me, or Mother. I think of Degas. She's with him so much now, and certainly she admires his painting immensely, and she's learned from him, about color, and angle, and brushwork, and capturing the ordinary life.

The picture holds more than all this, though; it's as if May painted it as he looked over her shoulder.

v.

As I sink into the green chair again, taking up *le journal*, May says, "You look splendid today, you know, Lyd."

"Thank you. Maybe it's your eyes."

"*Mais non*, anyone would agree with me, Lyddy. You've always been beautiful."

As I find my pose, I think about how, when I first met Degas, he gave me the impression of an intelligent but fierce dog—well-dressed and utterly *comme il faut*, but a dog nonetheless. He bit into subjects—the foolishness of one artist or another, the insipidity of someone's latest effort, I can't remember—and all the while his eyes lit on things in our apartment, with an air of studying and maybe breaking them: the tea set, the Japanese vase on the mantel, me. I felt sure that if I opened my mouth, he would pounce. It's a kind of brutality.

And yet, something else emerged as he asked me questions. "Had I begun to feel better?" he asked, and "What was I reading?" When I told him, "Jane Austen," he looked curious. "Ah, *lequel*?" "*Persuasion*," I said, and then, surprisingly, his eyes lit on mine. A feeling connected us, quickly and with an absorbing depth. I wondered what he felt. In allowing myself to look at his face, which had seemed so arrogant and almost ugly a moment before, I discovered a sadness, maybe, or a sense of pain. It was as if I had rounded a corner, in a strange city, and had come upon a scene of terrible intimacy: a man weeping, a child ill. Yet, before I could think of something to say, the city rose up before me again, with its elegant avenues and public spaces, its overwhelming buildings, looming, sharp-edged.

I wonder about May, for she seems to welcome his presence. Certainly, he seems to have made of her—and of me too—an exception, and yet this sensation of being protected from the Cyclops by the Cyclops himself, while he eats everyone else in sight—well, it's fragile at best. And he does eat people, I know, one friend after another.

And yet I could see what he meant to her, from the beginning. His invitation to her, a year ago, to join his group of Independents, came to her as an invitation to live, to create the art she knew she could create. Her whole desire now is to have her début in the Impressionist Exhibition this spring.

At tea, on that first meeting, I saw something else. In the air between him and May, I sensed something bright and resonant. She smiled, and he bent toward her.

In May's studio, my arms ache again. May and I have been quiet for some time. I catch myself almost sleeping when May's voice cuts into the drowsy air.

"I might go to the Louvre this afternoon, Lyddy. Could you come too?"

"I'd love to, if I feel able."

"We could look at the Dutch collection again."

"*Oui.*"

"Maybe May Alcott will come with us. We can go by carriage, and fetch her."

May Alcott, Louisa May Alcott's sister, is married to a Swiss man now, so we see her much less, but I welcome our outings with her, and with our young and wealthy friend Louisine Elder. To go about Paris with this small crowd makes me feel young and careless, or, as careless as I can be.

Love comes, or illness. Last summer, my life changed, all in a day. After asking me questions, with his little pince-nez glittering, the doctor took May and Father aside to discuss my situation. Mother was ill then. When May returned to my room, her face a map of worry, I knew in a moment how bad it was, and I knew too how she would fight this truth, how everyone would fight it. I could not hear all of her words, because the world seemed to become unreal, as if I were miles away, looking through the small end of a telescope, just as I used to do with Robbie's when he got a toy one for Christmas one winter at Hardwicke. I would sit in the window seat, behind the curtains, and point the instrument out to the meadow, and at first I could see the horses so clearly that I could watch the breath coming out of their nostrils, and then I'd turn the telescope around, and suddenly the meadows, and the road, and May's snow castle, and the flower garden—dry sticks in snow now—would become tiny, a perfect miniature. Only this time, when May spoke, the miniature held her and me and my bed, in my room in Paris, and all around the world had vanished, and I felt myself too to have no substance, but to be made of air. Pain and air.

"Bright's Disease," she said, and I almost laughed, thinking how ridiculous that a disease of the kidneys should be associated in any way with brightness. "But, Lyddy, even a French doctor can be wrong. We must simply watch your diet, and keep you well rested. That's all there is to it. You must simply be careful."

But how can carefulness make this all right? It's not up to me. Heaven knows, I'm nothing if not careful. This illness is inside me. I feel that I live on a plank jutting out over an ocean filled with sea monsters. Sometimes I think I'm better. But maybe it's just that a pavilion has been created around my little plank, right by this ocean, sea monsters or no, and so much goes on in it—jugglers, singers, romance—that I am merely distracted and amused.

"Lyddy, did you hear me?"

"*Désolée*, I must be daydreaming."

"I can tell! I have to pull you back, Lyd, right back into that chair. You left me quite alone there, for a few minutes. Where did you travel to?"

I smile. "Oh, well, I go anywhere I wish, May: Pennsylvania, Germany . . ."

"Not Germany!"

"Actually, I was probably thinking simply about our apartment, and lunch."

"Lunch can be an absorbing subject, I know."

"Yes, and that pattern for a new gown."

"Another absorbing subject."

I can't always tell May my thoughts, because she can't bear to face illness or death. My whole family's like that.

I think May's sadness, when she heard my diagnosis, was increased by her memory of earlier sorrows. The doctor, even,

Woman Reading (Femme lissant), Joslyn Art Museum, Omaha, Nebraska.

may have reminded her of other doctors, like the fat German one in Darmstadt, who looked at Robbie's legs, and told us there was nothing seriously wrong with him. All we had to do, he said, was to make Robbie exercise with regularity, and take some medicine to strengthen his bones. For awhile we could all look at each other as if the world were an ordinary place.

But if something comes to someone, and makes of their body a house to waste and gnaw at, doctors can do nothing, and love can do nothing either. The baby, George, died too, only a month old, when May was just beginning to walk, and, before I was born, the baby girl, Katherine, named for Mother. Once the youngest, Gardner, came into the world, three years after George, I could hardly bear to look at him, for fear he too would be still and cold.

"I think that'll do for today," May says. I can tell she's pleased with her start.

I rouse myself, and shake off my thoughts. To be in May's studio, now, in Paris, and not in Darmstadt, or in Pennsylvania either—to have come this far—well, it's lucky.

"May I see?" I ask.

"It's only a start," she says, and I look at a swath of white paint—the *fichu* around my shoulders—and the beginnings of a woman's face, in profile, the nose and mouth painted with delicacy, the eye a darker line, and a sketchy band of brown for her hair, whitish-pink broad strokes for her cap.

Something about this woman, half-suggested in oil, makes me bend toward her. *Who is this?* I ask myself, for I can't think it's me, and yet I know, with exquisite pleasure, that it is.

vi.

As I sit in my armchair, reading Flaubert, later, the image of this woman, the one May is painting, comes to me again and again. I discover a yearning to be close to her, to be present as she comes closer to the surface. It's like watching someone swim toward you, only it's much slower, and you see her at first underwater, a moving blur, and you wait for the moment when you'll see her arms, and then her face, her hair streaming wet in the light.

I could never confess this to anyone, and I can barely even think it, but I'm aware too of another sensation, the feeling of May's eyes on me, as she painted this morning. Do other women have such feelings? It isn't that I feel beautiful. It isn't something outward or visible, really, at all.

Such sensations make me think of my girlhood. I look closely at each memory, in my own gallery, as if to discover some clue, some fresh element in the story: a hand on an arm, a glance, a glove left on a seat, maybe. It still surprises me that I never married.

Of course marriage isn't the solution to all of life's ills. It can bring boatfuls of ills, if one is unlucky—think how unhappy people can be, yoked together. That's what I admire about Flaubert, how he sees that, and makes even the dullest marriage into an interesting story. He creates poor Emma Bovary, full of restlessness and vague dreams, romantic wishes, and here she is (I'm halfway through), caught in life's meshes already, an absurd marriage, an impossible love affair.

How does one go about this business of living? I dwell on this question often, now. One's life looks different, terribly sharp and clear, when one begins to comprehend the fact of one's very particular, looming death.

vii.

Sitting in front of the mirror in my nightgown, brushing my hair, I look younger than I feel, as always, although I can see, these days, hints of the old woman I might become, if I'm lucky. I study my fine crows' feet, the shadows under my eyes. My hair, in waves, looks reddish blonde still in this lamplight; only in the day can I see the change, especially at my temples, to white.

In bed, with the lamp out, I find myself remembering the War at home. It still feels fresh to me, the tearing up of our cousins' land in Gettysburg, the long and bloody list of young men who entered the fight: John Chandler, James Endicott, Andrew Lyman, handsome William Dabney. At least Robbie was spared such a challenge. And when I heard of another death, of someone young and fine, I felt another door close inside me, a breeze blowing it shut. I had written letters to each of them, attempting to sound cheerful, as if the world had not opened up a hideous wound, and as if they were not positioned to fall, limbs blown off, chests yawning red, their horses foundering in the mud. We urged Aleck to hire a substitute, and thank God he did, or he too might be bones, like our cousin Frank. It isn't fair, Heaven knows, and Aleck will carry the knowledge with him all his life, but look at him now, vice president of the Pennsylvania Railroad, with wealth and a full, rich life, a country house, a fine marriage, four children.

And Thomas Houghton, whose eyes were the color of hazel, and who almost brought my hands to his mouth, who kissed me one summer night in West Chester, moulders now beneath Pennsylvania soil.

All those lives, all those lives, and I felt my life too whisked away, in the shot of a cannon, the tearing apart of flesh from bone, heart from rib, my brains blown and scattered into a thousand pieces, the green fields turned to blood and muck, my life over at twenty-seven, for how was I to live, then? To live, afterward, I thought at first, was to walk always on graves, hearing the whisper of ghosts. Not Robbie's ghost only, now, or the babies', but thousands of others too, and in my dreams each night I'd see a meadow of men, mowed down, moaning, and I'd look into the face of each, searching for one face, and sometimes I would find that face only to see it crumble, or shatter, before I could touch it.

I wake frightened, and for one wild moment, seeing only dark, I have no idea where I am: *in the root cellar at Hardwicke? In Germany? In West Chester? In the new house we built in the country, when I was twenty-three? In Allegheny City, when I was little? Yes, in Allegheny City, in our maid Cora's room, at the top of the house, her face impossible to see in the darkness—or else on the sleeping car of a train, hurtling somewhere headlong off a trestle into a river thick and black as tar.*

I try to think about something calm: the new picture May's

painting of me reading, or the apples and honey Aleck has promised to send to us from the States, for Christmas.

Restless, I come to the memory of the summer when I was twenty-two—a good memory, this one is; maybe it will help me sleep. It's of the summer day Thomas came on a picnic with our cousins and us, to a lake. We were living then in our new house on Olive and Fifteenth, in Philadelphia, and we took the train to the country, and hired a carriage. Once we arrived at the lake, we spread out our baskets: eggs, a big jar of sassafras tea, apples, biscuits and honey. After we swam, we sat on the blanket and ate our fill. Thomas looked at me often, and after lunch we walked together up the slope. He brought a book out of his pocket— Emerson's essays, wasn't it?—and began to read. *Maybe this is what marriage will be like*, I thought: *to sit together on a hill, in Pennsylvania, looking at the edges of a lake, now blue, now greenish gray, and to read to each other, thinking of large things—of Nature and Spirit—as we sit wrapped, rapt, in a cloud, a net, of affection.*

My ceiling grows a dusky blue with dawn approaching. Of course I knew, even then, that marriage was more real, more difficult, than a romantic afternoon. I had seen all that Mother had been through, with so many moves—once every year or two, often, difficult even to chart or remember—and her children's ill health, and her own fragile health, and Father's restlessness and impatience. But I found it hard to imagine my future in fuller detail, with Thomas half-leaning next to me, his hair still wet from his swim.

And when people see me now, what do they see? Certainly they can't know about a lake in Pennsylvania, or how a young man lay on his back, pulling me toward him, after reading for an hour while clouds scudded south.

viii.

Only the second day of modeling, and this picture is halfway done. I'm surprised by the urgency of my wish for this to continue: my sitting here, in this chair near the window, the lamp just over my shoulder, May painting, and the whole world at bay. Perhaps May feels something like this too, for she teases me now about my new profession.

"Be careful, Lyddy. You're such a good model, I'll find it difficult to let you go."

"Nonsense," I say, but I can't help smiling.

I asked May after breakfast this morning if I could pose with a book today, instead of the paper, and she agreed, as long as I read to her, and hold the newspaper again when she asks me. She added, "I'm not in the mood for Flaubert, though!" so I've left Emma Bovary at home, getting her thin boots muddy as she slips across the meadows to her shallow lover's *château*. I've brought my Wordsworth instead.

May asks for "Tintern Abbey," so I begin: "Five years have passed, five summers, and the length / Of five long winters." A splendid poem. It deepens as I grow older.

After I finish, May says, "You used to read that to me."

"Did I, May?"

"Yes, in Germany."

"I remember. I tutored you and Robbie, didn't I?"

"Yes," May says, but then she's quiet. She doesn't like to talk about that year.

When Robbie died, May was inconsolable. How old was she? Nine, ten. Ten years old, that must be right, because it was on May 24th, in '55, that he died; two days later, her birthday came and she was eleven. So I was almost eighteen.

She didn't touch the little cakes I'd bought. None of us seemed able to remember how to celebrate, even in the smallest way. I gave the cakes to the maid, and she thanked me for them.

It is at the funeral, in a cemetery in Darmstadt, where the minister speaks in

German, and cherry trees blossom up and down a slope, that May begins to cry. I try to embrace her, but she runs down the hill. I follow her to a cherry tree, covered in white blossoms. She stands near the tree, shaking and sobbing, and then she begins to hit the trunk with the side of her fist. "He was going to take lessons in drawing with me, when we got back to America. He said so. We were going to share a pony." She hits the tree with each sentence, pushing me away as I try to catch her arm and hold it. "I hate him for dying. He had no right to die."

I gaze at the page.

On the banks of this delightful stream / We stood together.

ix.

"I think it's almost done," May says now. "I think you'll be happy."

Bending toward the painting, I'm caught by its beauty. She's added a cloud, a light of pink, rose, around the edges, which surely hadn't been here, visible, and yet she's made something splendid with these colors. The woman reading seems suffused with rose. She holds a sheaf of papers, and what she reads seems to have dissolved into gray and pink and white.

"*Alors?*"

"It's lovely, May. Lovely."

"You like how the light's coming?"

"*Oui.*"

"I think the colors have turned out well—the dress has been worrying me."

"The colors are splendid."

May turns to put away her oils.

"Maybe one more day," she says.

X.

May hurries to the studio this morning, and I walk as quickly as I can. As we reach the place Pigalle, and the outdoor tables at the Nouvelle Athènes, she grasps my arm and slows down.

"I'm like a race horse today, Lyddy, aren't I?"

I have to laugh. A race horse is just what she is, fine-tuned and restless, bolting for the finish. I glance across the busy *place* at Le Rat Mort, wondering whether Degas might be holding court today. Usually he waves to us, or rushes out to greet us. But Le Rat Mort shows no sign of him. I see only a couple of young men at a table, laughing, and a *vendeuse* gazing into the street, cradling a cup of coffee.

In her studio, May opens the curtains, and light swings into the room.

"Did you sleep well last night?" she asks.

"Quite well," I say, as confidently as I can.

"You feel quite well today?"

"Yes, May, quite well."

"I walked you here too fast, didn't I?"

"The walk was lovely."

"Have to keep you healthy, Lyddy. My best model."

"Mais non," I say, but I think to myself, with hesitant pride, yes, I am, I am quite a good model, and as soon as I think this, I chasten and mock myself, sending my thousand little bees to sting me, and sing their disdain: *How could you think,* the song always begins, and the thousand bees hum and mumble and murmur into my ear, adding new verses as they find new places to thrust their stingers in. *All you've done is sit here,* they hum, *and you're not even pretty, you're pale as a ghost and a bag of bones too,* and then the fiercer ones sing, *She's changed you into a figure of beauty, through oil and canvas, but how can you think she's pictured you as you really are?*

I'm used to these insects. I seem to own them, after all. They occupy a special place on my acre, complete with bee-boxes I myself seem to tend, in my veils and gloves. I'm their queen, as much as I'm the sorry object of their attacks. They fatten on my clover and apple-blossoms and honeysuckle, and they practice their songs in the warm sun on my meadow. So I can't blame anyone but myself when they come to sting.

"I think Degas might come by today, Lyddy." May says this carefully, for I know she thinks I'm shy around him.

"Ah."

"He's eager to see the painting."

"Mm."

"He likes you very much. Only the other day he asked after you. He thinks so highly of you, Lyddy."

"Certainly he likes what he knows of me," I say. But I think to myself, maybe he's like my bees made visible? Can't May see how he could sting?

"He has been telling me he'd like to paint you one day, in fact."

"You must be joking, May." I almost slip out of my pose, to look at her.

"Why would I joke about that? You're a splendid model, he sees that." She adds, "He hopes to paint me, too."

Now I can't help breaking my pose to stare at May.

"You would pose for him?"

"Actually, I already have."

She has pulled her stubborn look, like a veil, over her face.

"Don't look so shocked, Lyddy. I don't show a bit of flesh, you know."

She's teasing me now; she pushes me to my limit, and then she smiles, her impish smile, polished to perfection since childhood, and I can't tell if she's making a fool of me or not.

Her face softens.

"*Ne t'en fais pas.* I've only modelled once or twice, Lyddy. Really, it's nothing to be worried about. He just needed someone to understand the pose, and I happened to be able to help him, when his other models couldn't."

"His other models?"

"You know what I mean."

"I'm not sure I do."

"Don't be so old-fashioned, Lyd. It's utterly *comme il faut*. Look at Berthe Morisot; she often sat for people, didn't she? She sat for Manet."

"Yes, and look at the women who are ruined by such men."

"Ruined! Lyddy, you sound as if you're in a novel."

"There's nothing fictional about it, May. It's ordinary life."

"Well." May looks at me soberly. "All I was trying to say was that Degas admires you."

33

"I am overwhelmed with gratitude."

As I move back into my pose, my head begins to hurt.

xi.

As the clock ticks the seconds, I find myself remembering the little girl who posed for May last spring, sitting in the blue armchair. I met her only once. She was shy and polite, the child of a friend of Degas.

How can I describe my uneasiness? It's just that, observing her, I saw freshly how a child has little real say about what happens. If my sister suggests she pose, so, and if Degas suggests she pose, so, and the child attempts to do what these grown-ups say, well, I suppose that's a child's life. And if the pose is indelicate, well, who is she to say so?

When the girl and her father left the studio that day, I attempted to bring this up with May, but she became furious and would hear none of it. *"Could you not move her legs closer together?"* I asked, in a gentle way. *"Oh, Lydia, how can you be so—American?!"* May exclaimed, her face growing red, just as it used to do when she was little. *"I am thinking simply of the child,"* I said. *"But what of the*

34

child, Lyd? The child is all right, she thinks nothing of the pose. Stop being so puritanical!" I felt my face grow hot when she said that, for I thought she might be right. I can't help having grown up in America, and I know May had to leave all that if she was to become something more than a lady portraitist or engraver. Yet I felt shame and anxiety for the child's situation. *"The pose is natural,"* May urged. *"She might loll in a chair like that at home. Who's to say a little girl should sit up straight, her hair brushed?"*

But May was deliberately misconstruing my meaning. To see those young legs, spread so widely apart, her arm bent back as if she were offering herself up as a small odalisque. May should have paid more attention. The child was not, after all, being painted by Degas.

Maybe my questions lingered in her, for she chose not to try another pose like that one. She even declined to have the little girl as a model again, although the child's father asked her many times. I've wondered, since then, if May herself began to feel apologetic toward the child, to have made such use of her. Not that she would ever say as much to me, or to anyone. She likes to feel she's right.

May confessed to me later that she'd allowed Degas to work on the background of that picture. I might have guessed, because of the strange cutting off of the chairs and windows by the picture's edges, and the dream-like proliferation of blue, flowered arm-chairs. Instead of one chair, three appear. A couch appears too, covered in the same blue material, not like any couch May owns, and all these pieces of furniture, placed at odd angles to each other, make a tense, unhappy family, having nothing to say to each other. May probably painted most of this, but I sense Degas' presence. He has a way of making a picture stirring and strange, like an unsettling dream.

She told me hesitantly. *"He helped me today."*

"Helped you?"

"He helped with the background."

"Did you ask him to?"

"I was surprised," she said, *"but I felt flattered."*

Flattered! This was May talking, fierce and independent May! "Well, do you like it better now?" I asked.

She looked at me then, a long, intricate look, and finally she said slowly, "I think he's added a certain brilliance to it, yes, and an unusual feeling."

"I know he's brilliant, May, and he paints unusual pictures. It's just that that painting is yours."

As we walk home this afternoon, arm in arm, I think about how I've created something with May, something that was not on earth before. As the crowds along the boulevard Rochechouart jostle us, I think I could fly home instead of walking.

Sitting in the lamplight, I try to read about Emma Bovary, whose life has swung terribly out of control, but all I can think about is May's picture. I miss something now, I'm not sure what. Maybe it's the posing I miss, or maybe it's the woman herself I'm missing, the one in the picture. I wish I could ask her a question, see her look at me. She has her own world now, a quiet and enchanted place, small and pleasant, composed of a few simple things: a chair, a newspaper, light. Sickness holds no place there. All is rose and white and cream, the gorgeous and simple here and now, the shimmering surface of things.

Yet at least she's safe. May has placed her in a world apart from the sting of bees and sickness, mortal life.

May has just asked me about my wishes. It's our old game. Each of us can say three. May's are easy; I could have spoken them for her. "To become a famous and brilliant artist; to make lots of money; and to own a *château* to which all of us can retire in style." You don't have to tell the whole truth, in this game; half or less will do. I know some others of May's, I think, the ones she can't say, something about how love could still come to her, in some astonishing form, on the glint of a wing, cutting through air, and how those she loves—her sister, for instance, and in a different way, the terrible Degas—could hold the course.

She leans on my knees, looking up at me with a comical face. "And your wishes, Lyd?"

I think for a moment. "To become a famous and brilliant model," I say. ("Oh, I promise you that," May laughs.) "To live well, I mean mindfully. And"—I hesitate—"to have as much health as possible."

"Oh, make that a bigger wish, Lyddy," May says with sudden fierceness. "Say, 'To be utterly healthy, for fifty years at least.'"

"Touch wood, May," I say, and I think how health is only the beginning of my most ardent wish. *To live in that world you made,* I wish to say, *that creamy world of no difficulty, no blood. To know another's touch, and to have children of my own, like Aleck's, and a life like a shell curling in on itself, glistening and clean on the sand, rolled in salt water, rolled and rolled, spent and spending.*

May brings her face closer. "Model for me again."

38

Tea

I stand in an unmown meadow, green-gold, rimmed with dark green woods. I'm looking in the high grass—for what? A ring? A bracelet? I look at my hands and see I've forgotten my gloves

A raft of clouds, the line of trees darker

i.

This morning, the place d'Anvers looks covered in feathers, all shades of yellow and green. May and I walk up to the boulevard Rochechouart, through the cool air, and then the boulevard Clichy, past the cafés and boutiques. I'm wearing the dress I bought at Worth's before Easter, as deep pink as the inside of a conch shell. Whenever I'm about to pose for May now, I feel as if we've created a new holiday; I imagine marching along with banners flying.

In May's studio, I enter the pose she decided on yesterday. I hold a gold-rimmed cup and saucer in the purple-and-black striped satin armchair, near one of the long windows.

Looking through this window, holding this cup and saucer, I contemplate a slice of blue sky above the gray building opposite May's studio, a sheet of light clouds moving slowly. Near me, I know, hover white and grape hyacinths, although I can see them only out of the corner of my eye: a gift from Degas. I breathe in their scent.

May's skirt makes a rushing sound as she moves. I cherish the way the room fills with quiet, like a bowl filling with milk.

ii.

When Degas rings the bell, and a moment later bursts into the studio, our calm scatters. As I move out of my pose to greet him, I note his energy and elegance. His walking coat is the color of sand. He looks almost handsome.

"You're beginning a new one?" he asks in a moment, looking at the canvas.

"We began it yesterday," says May.

Degas studies the picture.

"The composition's all right."

"I'm glad you think so," May says wryly. She turns to me. "Shall we begin again, Lyd?"

"Certainly, May." I lower myself into the chair and pick up the cup and saucer. May touches my hand to bring the cup an inch closer to my face. "*C'est bien.* Just like that."

"The line of the arm—," Degas adds. "Well."

"Well?"

"*Et bien*, you might wish the angle—just there—of the elbow—
to be sharper."

Looking out the window, I picture May standing next to
Degas, her head cocked as she looks at the painting, and at me.
He's quick to make suggestions. He can make jokes at her
expense, too, as he does with other friends. Once he told her, in
front of me, that something she'd just painted—an oil of a young
woman in a theater—looked sweet and bland, like an English tri-
fle. "One might like the first taste, but then, after a moment, one
longs for something more—what?—nourishing." May retorted,
"I think it's nourishing enough, thank you." She is not easily
thrown off balance, although, in the privacy of our household,
she sometimes lets me see how furious she is at him, or how dis-
tressed she feels by one of his remarks.

"If you were to move her arm just—so—you could make a
more unusual effect."

"I like the angle of her arm. I think it works well."

"Oh, well, of course if you like it."

"I do."

45

Once May begins to paint, I hear Degas light his pipe, and I smell the pungent tobacco, as the pigeons whirr and the light in the studio grows brighter. I'm surprised he's staying so long today, and I'm not wholly happy. His presence changes things. For one thing, May becomes more self-conscious and alert. And I suppose I'm jealous of her attentions to him.

"Have you seen the reviews of our exhibition?" he asks May.

"Yes."

"Most of the critics are idiots."

"You come across rather well, though," May says. "Huysmans adores you."

Degas gives a short laugh. "Yes, and what did that elephant Ephrussi write? My subjects are 'bizarre,' the features of my dancers 'repulsive'?"

"He said more than that. He praised your drawing."

"Oh, well, then. I'm much in his debt."

"All of it was harder this year, with Monet at the Salon instead, and Renoir too."

"The world is full of self-serving people, attempting to puff themselves up. What does art matter to them? If they want to parade in front of a stupid public, at the official bazaar, I have no need of them."

May isn't quite as irritated about friends like Renoir, but she too feels insulted, I know, by some of the reviewers of the 5ème Impressionist exhibition this month. They find her colors too dark, her pictures not as interesting as the ones she presented last year, when she made such an astonishingly successful début. Henri Havard claims her originality has dimmed. Philippe Burty thinks her drawing misses "tonal strength," which is ridiculous, and he even blames her for—how did he put it?—"aspiring to the partially completed image." "He simply doesn't like what I'm trying to do," May says, throwing the newspaper on the couch. "Critics can be such fools."

I know she faults Degas, in part, for the haphazard air of this spring's exhibition. She worked all winter on prints to be published in the arts journal Degas envisioned, *Le Jour et la Nuit*, only to discover a few weeks ago, right before the exhibition was to open, that Degas felt his own prints were not ready. And, because he was not ready, the whole journal was abandoned. She had only eight oil paintings ready for the show; so much of her effort had gone into her printmaking.

May felt angry with Degas, just as Pissarro and the others did. Yet she has not stayed angry. "After all, I could have painted more," she says. "I'll have to do more this year, that's all there is to it. I'll have the critics on their knees next spring."

As a girl, of course, she proved she could hold herself the equal of anyone, including Father, who has never been one to hold back his thoughts. He tried to prevent her from doing so many things: taking art classes in Philadelphia, studying and travelling on her own in Europe, living in Paris. He couldn't understand why she wouldn't simply stay in Philadelphia and marry. "You could keep painting, May. We do have some culture in America, you know."

She holds her own with Degas too. Something teasing and fierce is in their friendship. Although she acknowledges that his wit can be too caustic, she relishes it sometimes, and she certainly admires his intelligence and his devotion to art. All year, she has seen him almost daily, making use of his printing press, experimenting with various methods, brushing shoulders with him at his studio or hers, at museums or dealers, and of course at our apartment too. She even began to pose for him more often in the winter (*and May Alcott died just after Christmas*, the memory glancing into my mind like a bird, and flying off again, *her face pale, the infection from childbirth ravaging her*).

May still poses for Degas, probably more than I know. Of course, she's not like his other models. I've often been with her in his studio as she poses, looking into a mirror, trying on a hat, sitting with her folded umbrella. These pictures bear almost no resemblance to the others I know he's painting now, of dancers, their arms and shoulders bare, their legs muscular in tights. Awkward these figures are, ugly sometimes. He shows them in harsh light, from unflattering angles, laboring to raise their legs, or resting, exhausted from their labor.

I've heard rumors about other pictures he's working on, of subjects too risqué for public view. I wonder if May has seen them.

Looking out the window, for all the world like someone at a party, I hold a pretty, empty cup and gaze at the ribbon of blue sky. I watch quick brush strokes of birds, rich gray against blue, and listen to the subtle tones in my sister's conversation with Degas, the shadings, the slow move off into another color. *How close to May does he stand?* I wonder. *How do they look at each other?*

"You'll both come to my *soirée* this Saturday, I hope?"

"Of course we will, won't we, Lyd?"

"I hope so."

To brush shoulders with his and May's friends—Renoir, Caillebotte, Pissarro, and others—to feel alive in that bright, crowded space, makes a heady kind of joy. If the ticket of entrance is the risk of the host's acid wit, well then, I suppose I too am willing to pay the price.

"And I am hoping you'll sit for me again one day, Mademoiselle Cassatt."

"I'm honored," I say, holding my pose. This is at least a partial truth. The pleasure I felt, in modeling for him last January with May, surprised me. In his studio, he posed me sitting down, holding a guidebook. The idea, he explained, was that we were in the Louvre, possibly the Etruscan gallery, two visitors, one standing, one sitting.

How can I describe the sensation of being looked at by this man? His look felt, at moments, like a storm on a coast, stirring the trees to wildness, shifting the dunes. I hadn't felt prepared.

The thickness in the air of May's studio becomes palpable. I imagine opening my mouth to eat it like bread.

"I'm sorry, May. Did you say something?"

"Lyddy! I thought you were listening! We were just talking

about this summer. I'm encouraging Monsieur Degas to come out to the country to visit us, when we rent our house in Marly."

"Ah. Of course. That will be lovely."

"You must enjoy the country, Mademoiselle Cassatt."

"*Oui*. It can be so hot in Paris in the summer."

"Our nephews and nieces will be visiting," May adds. "Our brother Aleck will be coming over from the States with his wife and four children. My sister is eager to begin spoiling them again."

"I think we spoil them equally." I smile, just to think of them. I think of Gard too, on his own now in Philadelphia, a bachelor still. I long to see him. Outside the window, high up, the white-fleeced clouds have begun to come apart, into feathered fragments.

"And will you work there?" Degas speaks to May, his voice gravelly and low.

"I'll do what I can. I can paint outdoors, in good weather."

"Yes. I'd like to see what you do."

"You'll come and see."

"*Oui*. I'll come and see."

"Lyddy seconds my invitation."

"*Bien sûr*, of course I do."

The light has moved from my chair to the floor beside me, and soon, I know, it will become something diffuse, not pouring in these bands onto the parquet. It will become, more, a thought, an idea of light.

iv.

"Ready for a rest, Lyd?"

As I move out of my pose, I see my sister standing by her easel, looking exhilarated and tired. Degas lounges in the armchair nearest May, his eyes heavy-lidded, like a lizard's in the sun. He rises slowly to his feet, as I rise.

Looking at the painting, I see a woman, clothed in pink and white, the white (my dress's lace) making a brilliant cloud around her neck, and again at the opening of her sleeve, with a tumult of color (the hyacinths) around her head. I bend closer to the woman's face, her chin half-hidden in the whiteness, her forehead in the swirls of golden-red, her eyes, touched with quick strokes of blue, looking elsewhere, her mouth half-smiling, holding in her thoughts.

Look at me, I long to say to her. *Tell me, what are you thinking, as you*

The Cup of Tea, The Metropolitan Museum of Art, from the Collection of James Stillman, Gift of Dr. Ernest G. Stillman, 1922. (22.16.17) Photograph © 1998 The Metropolitan Museum of Art.

begin to bring this gold-rimmed cup to your mouth? Absurd, I know, this longing.

"*Alors?*" May looks at me, questioning.

"It's beautiful, May."

"Do you really like it?"

"Of course I do. The color is beautiful."

Can't you think of another word? I wonder. May is waiting for something more. I feel unable to tell her all my thoughts: how I yearn to be this woman, to be composed of this swirling, lovely world, not Lydia, not myself, feeling exhausted and cold suddenly, my head hurting, as Degas looks over our shoulders.

"Very pretty," he says.

"Pretty! Don't insult me."

He throws her a teasing, dark smile. "Oh, well, you know it's very good," he says. "You have an enviable sense of line. A woman shouldn't be allowed to have such a sense of line." He adds, "Of course, you're lucky in your model."

"The model has little to do with it," I say.

"*Au contraire.* A model has an immense amount to do with it." He looks at me with amusement.

"Of course she does. Lyddy, you're absurdly modest." She

points to her canvas. "I'm going to do more with the dress and the background, and a bit more with the face. I can't make you pose any longer today. And the light's changed."

"I can come tomorrow," I say, although my head is beginning to ache in earnest. My illness rushes back to me, sometimes, like this.

"Lyddy." I feel May's hand in mine. I have bent over, and someone has lowered me into a chair.

"I'm all right, May."

I feel her hand on my forehead, and then her fingers under my chin, untying my bonnet.

"Some water for her, please, Edgar."

"Of course."

Soon a cup is held to my lips, but I shake my head.

"I'll be all right."

And then I am inside my illness again. All that happens means nothing to me— the long walk out of May's studio to the street, the cab ride home. I am half-aware that I have ceased to care what anyone thinks of me, even Degas, who rides with us in the cab, looking strangely shaken.

V.

Days can be passed this way, lying in bed, shrouded in the duvet I love when I am well, and that now seems to rub and hurt, to be all wrong, just as the world is wrong in each detail. Sounds that could give pleasure to someone healthy seem to prick me until I'm a bloody mess: Lise placing the washing bowl on my table, Mother's voice calling to May, the clattering of silver and plates, Batty's yips, and, muffled but upsetting, the sounds of avenue Trudaine.

I am not fit for this life. I hold still, hoping the illness will decide to go away, leaving me empty and picked clean, a thin replica of myself, but at peace and alive, like small bird bones on a cliff, that miraculously begin to sing.

I call to Lise, or to May if she's home. My mouth opens and my stomach pitches and heaves. Mother comes too slowly, and I can't bear to ask her to clean up my messes. Lise is immature, and dislikes illness; she wrinkles her nose and holds her breath, sighing and making a show of taking the basin away. May's better, because she has courage, and backbone, but she cannot disguise her distress at my condition.

Why is it that I feel at fault for this sickness? Surely I am not at fault. In the midst of my collapse, I feel fury at my family, the way they tiptoe around me and look at me with hushed faces, as if I've already died; and yet, at the same time, they seem impatient with me. *Be healthy or go, choose one or the other,* I imagine them thinking, *we can't bear to accompany you further into this illness.*

vi.

May has become restless. She's lost days, nursing me. Often she has even had to bathe me, for I've been too ill to bathe myself. I worry that she's disgusted with my body, pale and ungainly, my breasts heavy, too intimate for a sister's hand, the washcloth moving here and there, *my body a place I wish I could leave, like walking out of our garden at Hardwicke, and slipping through the gate into the meadow.*

Yet I love to have May near. She's been painting and working, on prints, I think, each morning (*and who does she see?*), but she comes home midday now, instead of continuing. Sometimes she reads to me, and sometimes, when I'm feeling very sick, she sits on my bed and holds my hands. When we're both lucky, her presence makes me feel calm, and allows sleep to come.

I cherish time with May. But I do not wish to pay this price for her presence.

vii.

I wake this morning to see May in the chair next to my bed. Someone has opened my curtains, and the sun spills onto the far wall, and onto my embroidery frame. May looks tired and determined, her face framed by her crimson bonnet and royal blue silk scarf. She's wearing a light gray coat. *If I could paint you now,* I think, *this is how I'd see you, tired and luminous, your face half in shadow, the light around you changing the air to cream.* She begins to pull on her beige gloves, and to work at the pearl buttons. She glances at me appraisingly.

"You look better."

"Well, that's a blessing."

"You've worried me."

"I worry myself."

I watch her button the last button and smooth her coat. For a moment, I think of my body as a kind of landscape, across which

I can travel, checking the trees and roads, seeing whether the bridges have held during the tumult of this week. It feels like a luxury simply to have a thought.

In the midst of this calm, I remember the painting. How must it look, in the light of May's studio?

"What day is it today?" I could ask, what season? What year?

"Monday."

I try to calculate how long I've been sick. May seems to guess my thoughts.

"You've been in bed for five days."

"Ah. I'm sorry about the painting, May."

"The painting's almost done. It can wait until you're well."

I study her face. She looks pale, and the circles under her eyes look deeper. She has been up with me many times this week, in the middle of the night. *And am I at fault, then?*

"What will you do today?"

"Oh." May looks careless. "I have lots to do."

"You have another model?"

May looks at me quickly.

"I can always find someone." She gazes at me for a minute. "I won't be able to find anyone like you, Lyd."

"Nonsense."

"You know it's true."

She looks out the window.

As she leaves my room, I say, *"Courage, May."*

viii.

Being ill, one has lots of time to think. Too much time. One's whole life comes to the bedside, to pay a visit, welcome or unwelcome. At some moments, the visitor seems to be some monstrous and misshapen figure, crouched on my chest, refusing to leave and presenting picture after picture of all that I remember. I find myself sifting through my insults to others, to May when she was little, to Aleck, to Gard, and to Robbie, before he died. I remember too my sense of bereavement, waving to Aleck from the ship as it embarks from New York. He grows smaller, to the size of a dab of paint, and I feel that in that figure, almost invisible now, resides my own childhood. *Will you marry Thomas? he asked, as we sat on the kitchen steps together one night. I was twenty-three. Yes. Yes, I will.* And, strangely, May Alcott threads through these memories, unbidden. I picture her as she looked when I last saw her, her ill face framed by the white pillow, her eyes closed. For three weeks last December she lay in a coma, in her house in Meudon.

Such thoughts become part of my illness, entwining with my nausea and my headache—a whole ocean pounding in my head. Can memories hurt? Then these hurt. I feel at moments as if I'm in an ongoing dream of sickness and grief, yearning to wake up into a new day.

In the midst of my illness, I discover an urgent wish to pose again. As I lie here, absurdly weak, I long to enter May's studio, to hold the cup and saucer again, or a book, or anything.

To model for someone is always a surprise; you never know what they'll make of you. After I posed for Degas, last winter, he completed various pictures using his original sketch—etchings, pastels, some placing us in the Etruscan gallery, one in another room of the Louvre. Looking at them, I saw, with painful lucidity, how he might see me—I mean, how he might actually see me, outside of the picture. The way he had posed both of us had been comical, really. We looked like two tourists braving the Louvre. I sat to the side, the guidebook held up to my face, covering my chin, while May stood, insouciant, attractive, her curved back to the viewer, her umbrella at a sharp angle to the floor, appearing far more interested in her own elegance than in the incomprehensible and stirring art she faced.

Of course, May and I couldn't know how we would look, especially once Degas added the image of the Etruscan gallery. In the etching, May contemplated and I peeked at a splendid sarcophagus of a half-naked husband and wife leaning and looking out of a glass case, as if to gaze back at us. When he showed me this version of the picture, I felt offended, to see this timid woman, hiding behind a book, barely able to look at the sumptuous couple, lounging in their eternal bed. I know it's silly to feel offended by the way someone portrays me—after all, this was not meant to be a portrait—but I felt offended nonetheless. May just praised the etching for its sense of composition and line, and she laughed, unbothered, at the wit of it.

I wish I could have responded with May's self-confidence, with her love of the satire in Degas' art. She's right to respond this way. But all I could think was, *Of course. Of course this is how he must see me.* I found myself arguing with him in my imagination, a fruitless exercise, telling him, *But you're wrong, I'm not such a timid soul. Whatever I look at, I look at wholeheartedly and with as clear an eye as even you can turn on the world.*

ix.

When Mother comes into my room, I welcome her presence as a relief and a distraction from such thoughts. In the chair next to my bed, she sits quite naturally in the present, here in our apartment, knitting, reading the newspaper, writing letters to friends in America, and to Aleck and Gard. She enjoys my company, and makes few inquiries into my inner state. I join her on the surface, in this here and now, leaving the welter of my emotions out of the picture. As I talk to her, I fold up most of my nettling memories, wrap them in paper, and tuck them into drawers, as Cora and the other maids used to do with our clothes when one season turned into another, in each house we occupied. I look around the room, and out the window, aware of the light, the color of the sky.

"I'm writing to Aleck," Mother says, adjusting her specs. "I'm asking him whether your youngest brother Gardner has any thought of marriage in his frivolous soul." Her silver hair is in a *chignon* under her cap. Her rings flash small bits of color.

I embrace the thought of handsome Gard, and of Aleck's brood, Eddie and Sister and Robbie and Elsie. I remember how I held Elsie, the youngest, on the day of her birth in Philadelphia. Such a tight little bundle of flesh, her forehead silk. I put my hand in the basin of warm water, to wash the baby, *the bloody sheets, Lois a bloated and exhausted ghost of herself. Will she live? I wondered, frightened.*

"Elsie must be so big now."

"Oh, yes. Lois says she's a handful." Mother looks at me with a wry smile.

"The children will love the country."

Mother nods. "May will have to take them on lots of expeditions."

"She's been talking about showing them Versailles too."

"Versailles would be splendid. They can see the fireworks."

"Maybe May will paint the children."

"*If* they can sit still," says Mother. "You know May has no patience for wriggling."

Children are excellent medicine.

X.

I am awoken, mid-afternoon, out of a troubled sleep by May sitting on my bed. She's breathless from her walk up the five flights to our apartment. My dream disperses (*a soldier, his face blasted, my own hands red with blood*).

I rub my eyes and look at May, as she unbuttons her gloves, pulling at the buttons in her impatience.

"I've found a new model, Lyd. Actually, two."

"I'm glad," I say, although I catch another feeling before it tries to slip away: jealousy, is it?

"One of them is quite young."

"*Ah bon?*" My jealousy bites more sharply.

"Yes. And quite restless."

"Restless?"

"Wriggly."

I stare at May, and she laughs. "*En effet*, it's hard to sit still when you're under a year old."

"Ah." I'm aware of my relief. "You've found a child?"

"Our landlady's great-nephew. Her niece is visiting, from Dieppes."

"How did you ask them to model? You've asked the child's mother, too?"

"Yes." May looks very satisfied with herself. "I met them just outside Madame Phillippe's apartment. The baby lay asleep in his carriage. He has golden hair, Lyd, like a cherub, a Tiepolo cherub."

"I'd love to see him." My bedroom feels small suddenly, even smaller than usual, as confining as a hatbox.

"I'm sure you'll have a chance to see him. They're staying for a week with Madame Phillippe."

"Bring them up for tea, May."

"If you feel well enough."

"I'll feel well enough. In a day or two. I'm sure the baby would love Batty."

"I'm not sure Batty would love *him*. But I'll try to bring them up anyway."

xi.

This afternoon, May has brought a picture home, a pastel. Two figures, a woman and a baby, embrace, the child's arm tight around her neck. I'm amazed by the way she's shown only the delicate sides of their heads; you can't see their faces at all. The mother bends in, to kiss the baby, and all one can see is the line of the mother's cheek and part of her brow, the soft cheek of the baby. How astonishing, to place the kiss just out of our vision. It's as if May's saying, *this is something you can only imagine, for these figures have no need of you. Your look can only go so far.*

"How did you do this, May?"

"I had to get it down quickly, especially the shapes, and this line." She traces the soft "V" of the mother's cheek, cradled between the baby's small arm and head.

"*Mais*, how did you think of this pose?"

"I wished for two figures, so close they seem to mesh. I wanted the faces to be a mystery."

"I can almost feel the baby's cheek."

May is quiet for a moment. Then she adds, "I wished to create the sense of a moment of utter closeness. It's quick and spontaneous, but, in the painting, it holds, it stays."

I think of Degas' dancers, exhausted, hard at work, isolated from each other and from the dance master, or from the men who linger in hallways off-stage. Sometimes you see only legs, the torso cut off by the painting's frame, and often you find yourself in an odd relationship to his figures: spying on them, or looking down at them. The space between them is fraught, nervous. I can't remember seeing a picture of Degas' in which two figures embrace, right at the center, so close you could touch them, and I certainly can't imagine him painting a subject like this, so fresh and joyous, so spontaneous: a mother and a baby, utterly in love. The strength of the lines, the boldness of the colors and the design, is pure Mary Cassatt.

"I know of no one else who could have created this, May."

She looks at me, flushed, triumphant. "I know."

I look again at the pastel: the rich blue color of the armchair, the deep green of the woman's dress, the gold and white of the child's hair and chemise, the auburn of the mother's hair, the restless greens and reds of the wallpaper pattern behind them, the mysterious and gorgeous shadow, in red, between the mother's face and the baby's. The whole composition centers there, in that red shadow, in that ardent and unseen kiss.

I carry them inside me now, those two figures, holding each other in a fierce embrace. *Arm and arm, cheek and cheek, in a swirl of color and brightness. Two figures bending in to each other.*

xii.

Today I am well enough to be brought into the parlor, in honor of Isabelle's and Michi's visit. May has just finished her oil of them; I hope to see it soon. May says it's a bathing picture, in a *déshabillé.* She borrowed one of my white morning dresses, and the Delft washing bowl from my room. "You'll like this one, Lyddy," she says.

Michi in the flesh holds a chocolate éclair as he sits, happy as a drunken sailor, on Isabelle's knee. He's dressed in a Tartan frock with a white pinafore, and his little brown shoes seem to be conducting a frenzied, happy orchestra. Isabelle has a gentle manner. She listens politely to May and to Mother and Father, as they describe our nieces and nephews in America. I present Michi with a gift of little wool socks, and May gives him a new toy-book by Kate Greenaway.

"You'll be leaving for Dieppes soon?" Mother asks, in French, offering Isabelle sliced melon.

"*Merci bien, madame. Oui*, we leave tomorrow morning."

"Will you be coming back to Paris in the coming year, *madame?*" Father asks.

Isabelle smiles. "*Je l'espère, monsieur.* Only, our family may be growing larger this year, and you know, it becomes more difficult to travel."

Michi grabs a *marron confit* from Isabelle's plate, and offers it to Father. Father accepts with good humor. Batty sits on the rug near Isabelle, wagging his tail and looking up at Michi, hopeful that a *marron* or an *éclair* might fall to the floor.

Later, after the small company manages to bundle themselves out the door, all of us seem to feel momentarily bereft. Mother sighs and Father picks up *Le Temps* half-heartedly, throwing himself into his armchair. May walks up and down a few times, glancing into the mirror over the fireplace, and then gazing out the window on the south side of the parlor, her forehead on the glass: from that window, I know, she sees all of Paris. I open my book—*Sonnets from the Portuguese*, my old copy, dog-eared—and try to read, but all I can think of is Michi's plumpness and cheerfulness. I wish May had made dozens of pictures of him, so we could imagine him here.

May comes to sit on the ottoman near me.

"She was a good model, wasn't she?" I ask.

"*Oui.*"

"And the baby too."

"The baby too."

"You'll have the children to paint this summer," I remind her.

"*Oui.* You're right, Lyd."

"You're very good at painting children, you know, May."

"Do you think so?" May looks younger for a moment. She searches my face.

"I do. I most certainly do. You're brilliant at it."

"I was surprised myself, how well the pictures came out."

I glance at my book.

The face of all the world is changed, I think, / Since first I heard the footsteps of thy soul.

"The good thing is, May, you'll always be able to find wonderful models, in children."

May's face is hard to interpret. "Yes, Lyddy, that's true."

xiii.

It's like a gift, the oil painting, when May shows it to me: a calm moment, a mother squeezing a cloth in a blue and white basin, her hand large and strong, her other hand holding a sleepy child, legs akimbo, eyes half-open, gazing at her, her face bent to gaze back, her forehead touched with light, her morning dress a white landscape on which he rests, becalmed, idle, in this moment before bathing, so clear, so still, that it remains cut out of time. Always the hand hovers, poised, in the water of the basin, always the mother bends to her baby, always the baby bends toward her. Outside the room, the world moves on, with its ships and trains, its republics, its foreign colonies, its industry, its injustice, its wars, its terror. The world becomes merely a thought about something other than this quietness, this room, this careful love.

Elsewhere now, the bloody sheets, the baby's cry, the exhausted face, cherry trees on a hillside, dirt tossed onto a box of wood, agony and then absence.

xiv.

I'm better now, much better. Mother still thinks she and May should take me to one of the spas, perhaps to Pau, although Father blusters about needing them to stay with him in Paris, "and we've already sent the money for the house in Marly, May, I doubt we can get that back." I agree with him, although for different reasons. The thought of having to brush shoulders with hordes of English tourists, taking the water, is enough to make me ill again. And if I were in Pau for two months, I would miss half of Aleck's visit. I will have better food, and more peace and quiet, in the country with my family than I would at the baths.

xv.

On my second good day, May helps me into the deep pink dress again, and waits as I descend the stairs from our apartment one at a time. Mathieu brings our carriage to the front of the building, and we ride in style along avenue Trudaine to the rue des Martyrs, and up to the boulevard Clichy. The district looks bright this morning, awash with late spring. The air feels softer, and, as I step carefully out of the carriage, holding May's hand, a wave of satin holds me up, helps me move more lightly.

After the morning's brightness, May's studio looks at first a dusky blue, and I shiver. As May opens the curtains, and then the windows, light changes the color of the floors to a shiny wheat, touching the corner of the marble mantelpiece and turning it from dark gray to silvery blue. Even the farthest corners grow lighter, and this other world emerges again: the mahogany tea table, the plump armchairs, the folded throws and cloths, the cups and saucers, the Japanese vases, the Turkish rugs, the mirror over the mantel. The gold hands of the clock say a quarter to ten.

I almost laugh. What a feat! By some miracle, or God's grace, or astonishing luck, here I am again, in this room, with my sister, on a spring morning in Paris, about to engage in the creation of a concoction, a vision, made of oil paints on canvas.

And here she is still, the woman in the picture, holding her cup and saucer, about to drink her tea, a smile on her face, for all the world as if she is at a party, her dress a rich pink, the lace around her neck a spray of white water.

"Of course the hyacinths have gone," May says, as I sit in the purple chair. I look around. Of course. The high green table too is gone.

"Could you find more hyacinths, May?"

"I'm not sure. But it's all right. I like what I have of them."

She moves my chin, and touches my right hand.

"C'est bien. Hold that."

And I do. I hold the pose, in joyful relief that I am here to hold it. I welcome even the ache in my arms, the tingling in my fingers, the urge to move.

Illness has this edge of grace. If the illness lifts, even for a few days, and one can enter the world again, all things shine with clarity and value. This cup, so light, becomes a miracle. And how much more a miracle that my sister looks at this cup, and at me, and touches a brush to mounds of oil on her palette, and makes a design that places me at the center of her creation. I am indeed comforted.

The Garden

and then I see May, and she's small, only two or so, running through the meadow, and I catch her up and hold her. She's hot. She cries, "Baby." "There's no baby here," I say, running my fingers through her hair, and

Marly-le-Roi, septembre, 1880

i.

The garden hums. A piercing blue sky, and a hot sun, mid-morning. My gloves warm, as I hold my crochet hook and the blue thread.

"Lyddy. Could you hold your hands still for a while? I'm trying to get them."

I hold my hands still. I gaze at my gloves and the hook until my eyes begin to water. Keeping my head in the pose, slightly bent, I look up and to the side for a moment to see May. The lace of my white bonnet appears like an umbrella, held at a slant over her. Her white blouse looks damp, with a blue oil stain on the front. She frowns as she studies my hands. She is standing, dabbing her brush on the palette. I blink a few times, and look at my crochet hook, wishing I could make my next stitch.

"I'm in great danger of making your fingers look like sausages." May sounds annoyed with herself.

"Maybe they do look like sausages."

I glance at May's face again to see her smile, and then I gaze at my gloves, the color of tea with milk. I added the fine red stitching, in three lines, on the back of each one.

Soon my arms begin to hurt, and my fingers do feel bunched up, swollen, but my gloves and the day still shine.

"What are you making, Lyddy?"

"A shawl for Elsie's doll."

"Corabella?"

"Yes. Corabella." I picture Corabella's surprised blue eyes in her porcelain face, her bird's nest of flaxen hair, her porcelain legs and arms, with one of the toes chipped. One hand too has been broken, and Elsie insists on a new bandage every few days.

"Poor Corabella leads a difficult life," May observes.

"She is devoted to Elsie, however."

"*Oui.* Elsie is most certainly the sun and moon of Corabella's world."

This is an island, composed of May and me, her brush and my gloves, my aching and her gaze. On her canvas, I become a healthy woman in blue and white. Sun and brush heal me, brush and sun, and French birds in a French garden.

Astonishing, how this place—this garden, our rented house, the village—thrives, a short train ride from Paris. The Seine is a ribbon, waving through this countryside, out of the city. If I could, I would walk from Marly to Port Marly, or even to the bridge in Bougival, to see the river, as May has done sometimes with Berthe Morisot, who summers nearby. The air is good here. I've suggested to my family that we could live in Marly all year round, or in Louveciennes, but May feels too isolated in the country. She loves the rush of Paris, the closeness to galleries and to her friends. Degas lives only a quick walk from our apartment there. She has become restless, after three months in this village.

I find myself picturing a little house, all my own, full of books, here in Marly, snow on my pillowcase of a lawn, a small garden of flowers I like best, an armchair by a window.

Quick, light steps on the walk. At first I think it's Elsie, until I remember she's on the boat to America; Aleck and Lois sailed home with all of the children a week ago.

"Bonjour, mesdemoiselles, où est Batty?" Vivi hops in front of me, in a blue linen dress and a white pinafore. Her older sister must have come to help Mother with the mending.

"Pourquoi? Do you wish to play with him?" May asks in French.

"*Oui, mademoiselle.*"

"Run into the house and find him, and tell Madame Cassatt that I gave you permission."

"*Merci bien, mademoiselle.*" The child curtsies and runs to the house. Soon I hear Batty's sharp bark, like a small gold hammer—*tin, tin, tin!*—and the girl's high voice, as she tells him how they will go to the stream, and possibly see a fish or a frog.

Only a week ago Vivi played with Sister and Elsie near the roses, carting Corabella and Sister's doll Joanna in the wheelbarrow. Elsie brought me two handfuls of rose petals one day and asked if I could make something out of them for Corabella. "Petals are too delicate for needle and thread," I said, "and besides, they'll fade soon, and dry up." "Could you try anyway?" she asked. "Corabella likes roses, and she needs a new shawl too." So I shall surprise patient Corabella with this blue, lacy shawl. It will be getting colder in Pennsylvania soon.

I miss the children immensely. I almost say this to May, but I know she knows this. She misses them too, although of course she has her painting, and her friends. My longing for them is a hunger I cannot satisfy. I had not known I could love them this much.

Batty's bark is more distant. I think of Elsie, chasing Batty. She would squeal when she caught him, and he would wiggle and snap at her. If I were to paint Elsie, this is the picture that would first come to me. I could not comprehend her love of the difficult—of the very thing that spurned her.

"Elsie adores Batty," I say.

"Oh yes, and poor Batty is terrified of Elsie."

"Batty is terrified of nothing."

May laughs. "You know very well he's terrified of everything. That's why he barks so much."

I hesitate. "Like the person who gave him to you?"

May laughs. "*C'est vrai*, Degas certainly can bark." In a moment, she adds, "I think it's possible he can be frightened of his own bark. That is, on his good days. He can be kind, Lyddy, *n'est-ce pas?*"

"Certainly, he can be kind. He was kind to the children this summer," I say.

"Remember how he brought them *bonbons?*"

"*Oui*, he brought *bonbons*." I smile. "Is this our new litany, May? Shall we call it 'In Praise of Degas'?"

"I know he isn't a saint."

"A saint? No. I don't expect anyone of my acquaintance to be a saint."

"Well, what about you, Lyd? Surely you're a saint, if anyone is."

83

"*Mais non*, May." I look at her. "People always think a woman saintly if she's simply single, and not entirely self-centered."

"*Et bien*, I'm not entirely self-centered," May says, "and I'm single, and no one thinks of me as a saint."

I gaze at my gloves again, and the blue thread. "*C'est vrai*. Saintliness isn't the first word that comes to mind in describing you, May. Maybe it's because you have such ambition. I suppose a saint's only ambition should be to serve God."

"And your ambition, Lyddy? What do you desire in the world?"

"Me? I don't suppose my desires are much different from any other woman's."

May holds her brush in the air. She looks as if she wishes to say something, but then she looks at her canvas.

"I would have married, for instance, if I could have," I add. "Although I wouldn't call that my ambition."

"Would you have wished to marry, Lyddy?"

"Of course. If I could have married someone I loved."

I glance at May. She's looking expectantly at me.

"But, I remember, that year I began studying art in Philadelphia, someone asked you, *non*?"

"Who?" I look at her, puzzled, thinking of Thomas Houghton (*in the garden, at dusk, behind our West Chester house, his face glimmering in the*

84

Lydia Crocheting in the Garden, The Metropolitan Museum of Art, Gift of Mrs. Gardner Cassatt, 1965. (65.184) Photograph © 1993 The Metropolitan Museum of Art.

dark. "Lyddy!" I heard someone calling, from inside the house. I looked at him,
and the air between us seemed sweet and slow. "Lyddy!")

"The Harvard student, with the curly hair. You must remember, Lyddy, he fawned over you for months."

"Oh." I laugh. "You mean Joshua Winthrop."

"He was studying to be a minister."

"Yes. Oh, heavens, no, I could never have married him. Poor old Joshua, with the crooked teeth and the earnest smile. His idea of courtship was to offer me wise quotations."

"And your idea of courtship?"

"Oh, May."

"You brought up the subject, Lyddy. I was seven years younger, you know, and full of curiosity about you. You were so private. You never let me in on anything."

"I doubt there was much to let you in on."

"Oh, I don't know, Lyd. I would guess the opposite."

"Stop!"

"And what about that other young man, what was his name? The one from Virginia, who rode so well? He was handsome, I remember."

"You must be an elephant, May, you don't forget anything! You mean William, William Dabney."

"Yes. One of Aleck's friends. You sat in the parlor with him one night."

"Oh, yes, with my whole family walking in and out, not to mention old Nora, limping with her hind leg, and putting her nose into his lap!" *Quiet, William was, and shy, although when I looked up from something I was doing—currying a horse, weeding, pulling on my old boots—I'd see him looking at me.* "He was much too shy, May. It would have taken him five years to start a real conversation. And anyway, I was thinking of another by then."

"Was that Thomas?"

I am surprised at the way my throat feels thick, suddenly. I cannot speak. The blue thread wavers in front of my eyes.

"I remember one summer," May adds. "Everywhere I turned, there you were with him."

"Yes." *his hand touching my arm, my shoulder, his voice murmuring.* "Lyddy."

"Et?"

"Et?"

"What happened?"

I shrug. "It was so long ago, May. I'm not sure I can even remember what happened." *the air sweet and slow, threads thrown out between us making a fine mesh, pulling us in*

"You were engaged, weren't you?"

"Engaged. *Oui.*" *Slipping into the garden one night, in West Chester, after a day of swimming, we embraced for the first time, fiercely, hungrily, in the humid summer air, the rich, fragrant grass, with the sound of our dog Nora barking from the front lawn, children's voices calling to us, "Lyddy! Thomas!"*

My fingers feel numb, and the back of my neck aches. I sense the first signs of nausea, but I will it to hold off. How can I be no longer the young woman in the garden, wishing to be seen, and touched, my desire meshed with another's?

On that August day, Degas hovered behind May's chair as she sketched Elsie. His hand touched the nape of May's neck. He caressed her neck for a moment, and she leaned into him.

I listen to old Josephe rolling the wheelbarrow. The asters have come into bloom now. He's been weeding this morning, pulling out the straggling annuals, clipping the long pointed leaves of the irises. I have asked him if I may help plant the bulbs, and he's agreed.

I've told May that I wish to start a little garden on our balcony this spring, in Paris, because I won't be able to wait until summer.

"Oh, Lyddy," she says, "summer will come again before you know it."

"Lyddy?"

"Oui?"

"What are you thinking?"

"Oh, I was just thinking about gardening."

"Gardening?"

"It's amazing, how gardens help you understand each season."

"Except for winter, I suppose, when snow covers everything."

"Remember the snowdrops, by the front steps of Hardwicke, May, how they pushed up through the snow?"

It's like a dream I had, that August afternoon, here in Marly. As I walked in the garden, after lunch, I came upon something I could not at first comprehend. Two figures, one in dark trousers, a white shirt, blue suspenders, one in a yellow dress, embracing. The world bent closer, and slowed: the allée, *the summer leaves, the roses climbing the arbor.*

ii.

May's moving quickly now, brush to palette to canvas, and I resist the urge to move. To pose, after all, is to agree to a form of enchantment.

I hear Batty's bark, muffled through the trees and growing louder. Soon I hear Vivi running along the *allée*, and Batty scrabbling and barking—*tin, tin, tin*!

"You may rest, Lyddy."

I move slowly out of my pose, to see Vivi rushing up, flushed and winded. May bends to pick up her little dog.

"*Alors, monsieur*," she says, stroking his small head as he pants, "what adventures did you have with Vivi?"

Batty's eyes glitter as he licks her hands.

"He barked at a squirrel, *mademoiselle*, and almost fell into the stream."

May laughs. "Poor old Batty!"

She stretches. "Shall I release you, Lyddy? It's almost one. Father will be anxious to begin lunch, and your sister will be waiting for you, Vivi."

I stand up, trying not to wince at the pain in my back.

"When will Elsie come back to Marly, *mademoiselle*?" Vivi asks, taking my hand.

"Oh, soon. In a year, maybe," I say.

"A year! I'll be so much older then. Do you think she'll know who I am?"

"*Bien sûr*. She'll know you right away."

My back hurts, but I take a breath and feel Vivi's hand in mine, her fingers fine and warm. Vivi hops beside me as I walk, and we slowly follow May and Batty into the house.

iii.

At lunch, I do not feel well. Mother glances at my empty plate, and then at me.

"Are you all right, Lydia?"

"I think so."

"Have some of this superb *rillette*," Father says, offering me a slice.

"Thanks, no."

May offers me the bread, brought this morning by Vivi's older sister, and I tear off a piece. I like the feel of it, textured, dusted with flour on the crusty top.

Mother sighs. "It's quiet without the children," she says. She has said this at each meal since the children left. May and I glance at each other.

"Perfect day for renting a boat," adds Father. "Nice and hot. The children loved that, the day we rented the rowboat, at the pond in Louveciennes, eh, Kate?"

The children took turns that day. Eddie and Robbie went first with Aleck, while May and Father and I stayed on the bank of the pond and helped the girls feed the fat ducks and geese, and two swans. Once Aleck brought the boat in, May took Elsie and Sister out to the center of the pond. I can still see their broad-brimmed straw hats, the picture they made. It was a bright, clear day. The pond looked as blue as lapis. I sat on a bench under the willow, playing I Spy with the boys and Aleck, as Father read the paper and Mother dozed.

Aleck has become stiffer, more formal. Marrying Lois did not help. Poor old Lois, with her aristocratic American customs and her doughy imagination. And poor Aleck too; he's caught up in that cautious, smug world, most certainly. But with each day of his visit, especially when Lois stayed in Paris and we had Aleck all to ourselves out here in the country, he seemed to become younger and more carefree. That day by the pond, he took off his shoes and socks and waded, just as we used to wade in ponds at home, catching tadpoles. I had good talks with him, over morning *café*, and sometimes in the evening as we walked in the garden. His absence feels like the violent loss of some part of me: a rib, a lung.

"I think I might walk over to see Berthe Morisot," May says, "tomorrow or the next day."

"How is her daughter?" Mother asks.

"Very well, I think."

"She must be two years old now?"

"Almost. She celebrates her birthday this fall."

"Healthy?"

"Very healthy."

"We should make a quilt for the little one, shouldn't we, Lyddy? We have the perfect material, from those two dresses you don't wear anymore. I had been about to give them away."

I nod. I hold my sides, willing my illness to go.

"Madame Manet is very lucky," Mother says. "And her child's lucky, to grow up in the country, especially in the summers."

"Country children are always the healthiest," says Father.

"Is Berthe painting again, May?" I ask.

"She writes that she's done some of the child, and the nurse."

Mother looks as if she wishes she could say something to May. I can guess what it is, and I know she feels she can no longer address the subject directly to my sister, especially now that the picture has changed, with Degas often in the foreground. She used to urge her to think about marriage, to place herself in such a way that marriage could become a possibility for her, but always May would respond high-handedly, "I'm an artist. I am independent. That's the only way a woman can do it." "You could still have your art," Mother would say, ruffled. But she didn't think of May's art as something real, something genuine. She still finds it difficult to think of May as choosing all this.

Mother still has hopes, though. I know she would love to see May situated like Berthe Morisot—Madame Manet—married to a wealthy man, well-connected. Lois too enjoys such a marriage. Aleck has become so rich.

Father, of course, agrees, and yet, ever since the Impressionist exhibition last spring, when May's paintings sold so well in spite of the critics, he seems to have begun to let the thought go. I picture him on a shore, watching a ship ("*The Marriage of My Youngest Daughter*") sail away, just as my own ship sailed, and turning back to business. He looks at her, more and more, with simple admiration, of the kind he might feel for a manly acquaintance who's struck it rich, in railroads or in stocks.

"I can't imagine Madame Manet gets much painting done, with a small child around the house," says Father.

Mother sits up very straight. "Well, she has a nurse, after all. And she has only the one child."

"One is a handful, even with a nurse, you know that, Kate. Madame Manet certainly can't be working as hard as May does."

"I don't mean to suggest that she works as hard." Mother looks indignant. "I'm only saying, she's very fortunate to have a family, and her art too."

May sighs. "Well, she is fortunate, there's no doubt of that." She adds, sharply, "And May Alcott too was fortunate once."

Mother looks pained. She liked May Alcott, and so did I. *"This is for you, Lydia," she said, holding out a little sketchbook. "It has some sketches of you and May in it. I thought you'd like to have it." Her face a blasted winter landscape, stark white and shadowed.* May doesn't need to bring up her death so often, and with such bitterness.

"Bearing a child always carries a risk," Mother says, looking suddenly tired.

"A risk, yes." May tosses her head. "She could have become a very good painter, and then she got married, and look what happened."

I glance at May's face, furious and stubborn, and I think about how happy May Alcott was with her husband in their house in Meudon. Her baby Lulu lives in America now, with her Aunt Louisa, the writer.

"You're right, May," Mother says, "that did happen. But look at me. Five healthy children I gave birth to, and here I am still, an old woman, with healthy grandchildren."

Five healthy children, I think, *but one has been dead for more than twenty years, and another* (I put my bread on my plate) *is healthy no longer, and what about the two who did not live more than a day, or a month?*

"You never had the ambition May does, though, Kate," says Father.

"I had my own ambitions, thank you."

"Of course you did," he says, with compunction. He adds, "And you've been a model to your children."

Mother glances at him. "Well, I don't know about that. I just— it's just that having a family, and children, is natural, and good. It's a contribution in its own right." Mother's hands flutter above her plate. She touches her spoon, her white linen napkin, the asters in the vase.

I shift uncomfortably in my chair. Father shrugs his shoulders and breathes a noisy sigh, as May stabs at her salad and then lets her fork clatter onto the plate. All of us are as quiet as church, until Hélène comes in to take away the dishes and bring the fruit and cheese for dessert.

iv.

This afternoon, lying on my bed after lunch, the pain is mild, compared to last spring and other times, but I am terribly aware of my illness.

95

I look at the mound of books on the table. Mostly poetry, at the moment, especially that of May's friend Stéphane Mallarmé, but my head is sore. I can't imagine deciphering the words; the thought makes me nauseous.

v.

Two figures, so close I cannot distinguish them. A fabulous and strange beast, clothed and passionate. Can people's boundaries dissolve? I wonder, confused in that one slow moment.

vi.

May pokes her head around the door, and looks at me with dark eyes.

"Lyd?"

I create a smile for her.

"Yes, May."

She comes in and sits on my bed, close to me, catching up my hand. Her hands knead my fingers, as if she wishes to mold them like clay.

"You're all right?"

"Yes."

"Was it something you ate? Mother worries about the *rillette*."

"I didn't touch the *rillette*."

"You've been so well." She pauses. "Haven't you?"

"Largely, yes. I've been well."

"I know you've had trouble sleeping."

"May." I speak gently and slowly. "You know my diagnosis."

May looks impatient. "You've been fine, though, only sometimes with a little sleeplessness, and then—" She studies my face.

"I know doctors can do very little. But they're not wholly ignorant."

May twists her mouth just as Mother does. It would be comical to me, if I did not feel so sorry for her, and for myself, at this moment. I glimpse May's world as it will look when I am no longer here. I do not always feel necessary—in the grand scheme of things, I feel quite unnecessary—but the picture shifts when you look through the eyes of another. I see May, sitting upright, in front of her canvas, holding her palette and her brush, and looking at—air.

And as soon as I imagine this, another picture flies into my face: *in my place is another, some young woman dressed in a dress I might have worn. On her lap is Batty, or in her hand is a crochet hook, and blue thread. She reads, or holds a cup.*

May's stubbornness on the subject of my health begins to distress me more than my diagnosis. I feel sometimes as if I'm in a rowboat, all on my own. And this is all right, if I can still see land, and houses, and my sister and others walking on the shore. But to be cut off from the shore, to have only seabirds and the impersonal sun and salty waves to witness what's happening in my boat—this is too much.

"Promise me you'll remain healthy, Lyd."

"How can I promise what I can't control?" I say, bitterly, throwing the words at her.

vii.

The woman's head turns, and I see May's face—but how could her face have arrived here, in this arbor? I feel that I've become caught in a picture, or else this picture has been thrust into my face, and I must hold my eyes open to see.

viii.

After two days, my illness subsides and I'm able to pose for May again in the garden, crocheting. On the second day, at noon, she looks up and says, with satisfaction, "*C'est fini.*"

I've held off looking at the painting, this time, I'm not sure why. I'll miss this chair on the path, the garden around me, sunshine and insect murmur. Soon, these mornings in the garden at Marly will have vanished, just as the mornings and afternoons of the summer have already vanished, leaving only pictures in my memory. We'll be returning to Paris, and other people, our other life, more crowded and rushed, May darting across the city, to see friends, to go to a gallery.

"Do you like it, Lyddy?"

I look. May has created a calm scene: a woman in a garden, with a white lace bonnet and a blue dress, edged with colorful embroidery, and a dusky red row of plants behind her, leading up the *allée*, to the dark windows of the villa. She's crocheting something blue. And what is that double band of red on her lap? Ah, the sash of my dress. It startles me.

"Lyddy?"

"Oh, I do. I do like it."

May waits. I contemplate the face of this woman.

"The lines of the face—look as if they're dissolving."

"Do you like that?"

I try to smile. "Oh, May, it's magnificent. Yes. I'm amazed by those lines, her eyes, her mouth, how it's all present, and yet—"

I feel May listening hard.

"It's as if you've shown how fragile all of this is."

"All of this?"

I am embarrassed. I fling my arms out. "This garden, summer—"

May studies my face, and then she looks at the canvas.

I see something else, but I find it difficult to say this to May. *It's illness she's discovered.* I gaze at the shadows around the woman's eyes (*my eyes*), the muted color of her mouth (*my mouth*), the downturned lips. I comprehend how May sees her (*me*)—not what she acknowledges, perhaps, but what she knows.

"Do you like the light in it?"

"The light is fine."

"And her hands?"

"Yes, her hands are well done." I add, "It's a thoughtful picture."

"Thoughtful?" She moves closer to me, as she looks at her painting, as if to see it through my eyes.

"*Oui.* She's absorbed in her crocheting, but it's more than that. She looks as if she's looking inward. I suppose it's her eyes that make me think that."

May's cheek, hot and damp, touches mine, *just as on a hot Pennsylvania summer day, when she's small, and I'm carrying her somewhere. She's clinging to me, her face hot and wet on mine.*

May puts her arms around my shoulders and kisses me full on the cheek.

"Of course she's thoughtful. It's a portrait too, you know."

"I'm not so thoughtful."

"You're a contemplative, Lyddy. I've always known it about you. If you were a Catholic—God forbid!—you'd be in a nunnery."

I shake my head, but I picture with a rush of delight a cloistered garden, like the one we entered in the old *abbaye* south of Paris, stone archways, and a calm filled with something—if I were a nun I could call this thing God.

ix.

And, God in Heaven, what am I to do with this other picture, arriving in my life during one dazed moment in the middle of a summer afternoon in our garden in Marly? The woman is May—I see her face, her yellow dress. The two figures make a picture no one will paint, or see, yet it's framed, in a green like the green of the arbor, on the walls of my memory. I claim it for my own.

As May begins to put away her brushes, I catch one more glimpse of the painting.

The blood-red leaves lead to the dark windows, the red (*heart's blood*) on my dress a sash, a slash. How can May paint such darkness?

Maybe it's this talk about nunneries, but I feel a yearning for some sign—of grace, of a future life that holds more than darkened windows. Why should it be only Catholics who see such signs, like the girl who had the visions at Lourdes? I would be grateful simply for a dove, winging its careful way out of the sky. In the face of that wish, my own world seems suddenly spare and stoic and Protestant.

xi.

"Do you love him?" I ask her, as the shadows grow blue around us, once Degas has left on the train. It's August, and the air's still hot from the day. A scull passes on the river, with swift, long strokes, as the blade slices into the water again, and again. "Oh, well." I can just see her shrugging, tossing her hands into the air. "Do you?" I ask again. She hugs her elbows, and looks at the water, and then she comes closer.

"I'm overwhelmed by him."

"Do you intend to marry?"

She laughs and I think she's mocking me, but then she says fiercely, "I couldn't marry him, Lyddy. You of all people know that. How could I? He would crush my painting, me. I couldn't possibly survive it."

"Then what in Heaven's name are you thinking?" I ask, in anguish.

"I can't say what I'm thinking, Lyddy, but I can't bear to feel I can't have this in my life, ever. This is not Philadelphia. Am I to live with no feeling, like—?" Like you, she almost says, and I feel the cut of her words against my face.

"I'm not asking you to live with no feeling, May," I begin, and at once I'm aware how my own life must look in her eyes, a desert, parched under a hot sun.

Her arm around his neck, her face joyous

And—"Lyddy. You must try to understand."

xii.

As I stand now in the hot sun on the *allée*, contemplating May's picture, I almost shake with sorrow and fury. I don't want to give any of this up: May's cheek, this light, the possibility of love. How can this be asked of me? I'm only beginning to understand how to live. And here is May, her life in full flush, a success now, and healthy, and boldly independent. And she will continue, for years and years, after I'm no longer here. She'll ride her horse in the Bois de Boulogne, she'll paint and visit galleries and go to the Opéra and to Versailles, and in the summer she'll come back to Marly, or she'll go to the Mediterranean and feel the breezes, watch the water turn color through a whole day, a whole week, and she'll have her friends, and more than friends, for after Edgar Degas, she may love someone else, and embrace him in another garden, and even if I am a thought in her mind, a sadness, she will have happiness too. Her days glitter, round and new, like gold coins in a huge jar, filled almost to the brim, her only worry how to spend them.

May threads her arm through mine, and we walk toward the villa, my heart like hot sand. May carries her case of paints and brushes, and I carry my crochet hook and the blue shawl for Corabella, strangely heavy now for such a small thing.

"I have to live my life as it comes to me, Lyddy, I can't be always waiting. You can't know how it is."

But I do, I think. I do.

Driving

then I'm in a garden at the abbaye, and I see May, painting a woman in a yellow dress, and I call to her but she does not hear me,

i.

"But I can't believe she would sell it." Mother looks at me in astonishment. She's come into my room, after breakfast. I've just begun Henry James' novel, *The American*, and I put it down reluctantly.

"Well, it is art, after all. It's a beautiful painting."

This is the twentieth conversation I've had with Mother on this subject, ever since Moïse Dreyfus bought one of May's family paintings, the one of Mother reading fairy tales to Elsie and Sister and Robbie last summer in Marly. Our household has flown into a whirlwind of emotion over this, like a hen house visited by a fox. Feathers fly everywhere. In a larger sense, I think, May's recent success is the fox, or maybe May herself. The *6ème* Impressionist exhibition, which opened in April on the boulevard des Capucines, has been a triumph, especially for May and Edgar Degas. She's garnered excellent reviews, and has had offers on all eleven of her entries. People are saying she'll never have to worry now about whether she'll be able to sell her art, and at a good price too. "Too much pudding," May says, daily, about all the praise and attention, but I know she's delighted—more than delighted. Victorious.

"Yes, but Lydia, how could she sell her own mother, and her nieces and nephew?"

"She's not selling you! She's selling a painting of you! There's a difference, I hope."

"It's a painting of my grandchildren and me. How could she possibly think of earning money for it, and losing it to someone outside the family?"

I sigh. How, indeed?

"At least she won't be selling the three of you, Lydia."

I picture those: the one of me holding the cup of tea, and the one in the garden at Marly, and another one, a profile of me on the green bench in the Bois de Boulogne, with my black bonnet and the red trim. I look sober in that one, my lips a tight line, as May poses me looking off into the distance, with my coat a swirl of crazed autumn colors.

"Well, she's not selling them yet, at any rate," I say.

"How can you say that! Surely she'll never let those go."

"But art isn't made simply for one's family. It's for others to see too."

"Yes, and I wish others to honor her accomplishment. But she must honor our wishes also. A portrait of her mother should be returned to her family."

"I agree with you. I wish May would too. But she has her own point of view. She's an artist. She wishes her work to be out in the world."

"But it's a betrayal, Lyddy. Surely you see that. She betrays me, and you, all of us, by sending our pictures into the marketplace like this. Who is going to care about such pictures as much as Mary's own family?"

In the painting of Mother and the children, May shows them wrapped together in the beauty of the afternoon, the magic of the story. I have to agree, it's hard to think of that little band hanging on a wall in Moïse Dreyfus's house, adding to his collection. I had not realized the extent of May's ambition.

Yet I have become aware, too, of how I have contributed to her success. The pictures she painted of me have brought especially high offers, and immense praise. When people think of her art now, they think of me, although they may have no idea who I am.

May is home this morning, a Sunday morning. We've been making plans with Mother and Father for our move to a summer house in Louveciennes in a few weeks. Our younger brother Gard will be coming to visit, and I can't wait to see him.

"I have a new idea for you, Lyddy." May says this hesitantly, as she pours herself another cup of *café*.

"Tell me."

"A painting outdoors, in the Bois. With figures in a carriage." She looks at me hopefully.

"With Bichette?"

May laughs. "Yes, of course, Bichette. The carriage must have a horse."

"And—someone in the carriage?"

"Could it be you, Lyddy? I'm thinking of you, driving, with a little girl, and maybe Mathieu could be in it too, as the groom."

I try to picture this. I've seen some unusual pictures of Edgar Degas'—fashionable people near a racecourse. May has painted her own horse only rarely. "Who would the child be? Do you have a model?"

May looks into her cup. "Well, I know of one."

"Who is it?"

May looks at me quickly, her face flushing. "A little niece of Edgar's. Odile. Odile Fèvre."

"How old is she?"

"I think she's about five. She has a hint of baby plumpness still, and honey-colored hair."

"Her mother is Edgar's sister?"

"*Oui*. Marguerite."

"I thought Madame Fèvre had moved to South America?"

"Buenos Aires. She and Henri moved there two years ago. She's just visiting now, with her children."

"How many children does she have?"

"Five. Odile's the youngest."

"And will Odile come with her mother?"

"I think so, usually." May's flush deepens. "More *café*?"

"Thanks, yes."

As May pours the *café* into my cup, she studies my face. "So— will you pose for this one, Lyddy?"

The cup feels hot in my hands. I breathe in the fragrance, as I think about how I yearn to pose again, especially with this child. It's a kind of hunger. Yet I've been more under the weather than usual.

"My health has been so uncertain," I begin.

May interrupts me. "I know, Lyddy, *mais*—" She pauses, then adds, looking away, "*J'ai besoin de toi*. I need you. It's as simple as that. The picture I conceive of has you in it. Most of my pictures do, these days."

I look at May quickly, my eyes stinging. I am surprised, and moved, by her sense of such necessity. I realize suddenly that she must wonder, as I do, how much time I have left. And I realize too that I would regret each day I refused her. To refuse to pose is a form of betrayal. I study May's anxious face.

"And if I become sick while you're trying to paint me?"

"I'll figure out something. I'm very resourceful. Let's not court disaster, anyway, Lyd."

I taste the *café*, and add some milk, as I contemplate the difficult walk down five flights of stairs, the ride to the Bois, the long hours posing, the ascent, once more, of stair after stair. And I contemplate, too, the day I won't be able to rise from my bed.

"*D'accord*, May."

"Can you begin tomorrow?"

"Tomorrow. *Oui*."

iii.

This morning Odile comes to the Bois with her mother. May and I wait with Mathieu in a quiet part of the park, to the side of a gravelled *allée*. To our right is a stand of trees, and to our left, a large open lawn. A short drive would bring us to the café, and the lake, where children throw bits of bread into the water and sail their boats. May and I used to go there often on summer evenings for ices, with Louie Elder and other friends—May Alcott too, so pretty and happy. Colored lights threaded through the trees, above the noisy crowd.

Here, though, on this *allée*, all is quiet. Swallows skim the grass, and I spot a hawk too, soaring above the meadow. I wonder what it sees, with its sharp eyes: a mouse, a snake, a family of partridges?

The sun grows warm, and as I sit in the carriage I hold my white lace parasol over my head. May walks restlessly along the lane, shading her eyes now and again, looking for Madame Fèvre. Mathieu stands by Bichette, holding the reins and looking quite grand, in the black silk hat and frock coat May has borrowed for him, his ears sticking out, his fair face freckled.

After a while, a cab comes along, with two horses. The driver slows as he nears us, and in a moment a woman in a sherry-colored dress steps out, and then a little girl. The child wears a pink and white summer dress with short sleeves, and a black straw hat. Her hair tumbles in waves down her back, the color of taffy. May rushes to greet them. I see her bend down to talk to the little girl.

The girl holds her mother's gloved hand in her own bare one, and they walk toward me.

iv.

Posing in the carriage next to Odile, I think about how she has, not an ordinary beauty, but something more inward. She makes me think of Elsie, although Elsie would never sit still for an hour at a time. I discover something touching in this child's politeness.

May is talking to Marguerite, in French.

"Will you stay in Paris for the whole summer, *madame?*"

"I hope so, *mademoiselle*. I have missed Paris."

"And Buenos Aires? Do you like it there?"

"Buenos Aires is unusual. It's pretty, in parts. And Henri has found much to do, with all the new building."

"Your husband is an architect?

"*Oui.*"

"And your children—they like it too?"

"Do you like our home, in Buenos Aires, *ma petite?*" Marguerite asks her daughter.

"*Oui, bien sûr, maman.* I love my room there, and my parrot. And I love our orange tree."

Woman and Child Driving, Philadelphia Museum of Art: The W. P. Wilstach Collection.

"You have an orange tree in your garden?" I ask, wishing I could turn my head to look at her.

"*Oui, mademoiselle.* My parrot often sits in the orange tree. He says, '*Buenos dias,*' and he calls for me when I'm not there. He opens his beak wide and cries, '*Odile! Odile!*' He does not cry for my sisters, oh no, that's certain."

"Keep still, Odile! Mademoiselle Cassatt is painting a picture of you, remember!"

"Your parrot speaks Spanish?" I ask my companion.

"*Oui, mademoiselle,* Spanish and French. I am going to teach him English too."

"Better learn English yourself first, *ma chérie,*" Marguerite says, laughing.

"Oncle Edgar will teach me English, and then I will teach it to my parrot."

"I'm teaching myself English," pipes up Mathieu. I had forgotten his presence behind us, on the back seat, facing backwards. "I am going to America one day," he announces.

"And what will you do in America, Mathieu?" May asks.

"I'll stay in a hotel in New York, and then I'll go all across the country, to San Francisco, *mademoiselle.*"

"You've been thinking about this a lot, I see!" May says, and I can tell she's smiling. She likes Mathieu. "And what will you do in San Francisco?"

"I'll gaze at the Pacific Ocean!"

"And you will be happy?"

"*Oui, mademoiselle.* Very happy!"

"Ah, lucky Mathieu, to have such a dream!"

v.

I am aware of the day's warmth, and of Odile's shoulder touching my arm. My arms ache as I hold the reins and the whip. I wish I could take off my hat and my scarf.

As I pose, I wonder what people think of us, as they pass in their carriages or on horseback. When the *allée* is quiet, I can almost imagine that we're in West Chester, or at our beautiful old country house, Hardwicke. Looking at the lawn out of the corner of my eye, I can dream that it's the first meadow behind the house, where Aleck and I would ride. The *bois*, too, could be the woods around the rim of the pastures, dark and inviting, where we explored, playing wild Indians.

Clouds begin to enter the sky, at first just white ones, then tinged with gray.

"I hope it doesn't rain," May says.

When the sky whitens and the sun vanishes, the air begins to feel like cotton, thick and full. May tries to engage all of us in conversation, but her voice sounds oddly distant, and I am tired. Odile has become as quiet as a pond.

Odile moves slightly on the seat, and sighs.

"You must sit still, Odile," her mother says.

When Batty barks at something (*tin tin tin*), the child starts, and out of the corner of my eye I can see that she's turned her head to look at him. Then she says, in a small voice, that her head has an itch.

"*Alors*, take care of your head, then," her mother says, "but *vite, vite*! Mademoiselle Cassatt is painting an important picture."

"May I see it, *mademoiselle*?" Odile asks. I can tell she's removed her hat in order to scratch her head.

"*Bientôt*," says May.

The clouds cover the sun completely, and the trees bend in the suddenly cool breeze. I shiver, even though I'm wearing such a heavy dress, with a jacket, and my bonnet with fur trim, my long gloves.

"Perhaps the child is cold, May?" I say.

"I'm almost done for the morning," May says. She adds, "Are you cold, Odile?"

"*Oui, mademoiselle, un peu.*"

"Well, just a little more, and then you can chase Batty. Do you like dogs?"

"*Oui, mademoiselle.*"

When May releases us, Odile jumps off the carriage, and Batty runs to her, barking. She bends down to him, and lets him lick her face. Mathieu stretches, and takes off his top hat, loosens his collar. Marguerite smooths Odile's hair, and gives her a kiss, and in a moment we squeeze back into the carriage, laughing, and Mathieu drives all of us to the café, for *pâtisseries*. It's like a holiday, with Batty on my lap, May's canvas and paints stuffed under the seat, Odile on her mother's lap, and Mathieu, his silk hat cocked rakishly off his forehead, driving us through a tunnel of trees as the sun begins to shine again, in dappled patterns, on the *allée*.

On the second day of our posing in the Bois, the sky burns blue, and the sun shines with summer strength.

I am sitting in the carriage, fanning myself, with Mathieu behind me, when Odile arrives at our spot with her Oncle Edgar. She skips at his side, and when she says *"Bonjour, mademoiselle,"* to me, she smiles. She laughs when she sees Batty. Turning to her uncle, she asks, "May I give him something I saved from my breakfast?"

Edgar glances, amused, at May, and says, "Better ask Batty's mistress."

Odile shows May a tiny strawberry, half mashed from being held in her hand.

"Of course!" May says. "Batty adores strawberries."

"I thought so." Odile nods. "My dog adores them too." She tosses the strawberry into the air, and Batty catches it neatly in his mouth, eyes glittering.

"Now let's see about your hand, *ma petite*." Edgar draws a handkerchief out of his pocket, and rubs her hand briskly. "You're full of surprises, aren't you? I had no idea you'd been holding that strawberry in your hand all the way from the hotel."

"We're only staying in the hotel for one more week," Odile

confides to May, "and then we go to my Tante Thérèse, and after that to the seashore, for the air."

"How splendid," May says, setting up her paints. She drops a brush, and Edgar bends to pick it up. As he hands it to her, slowly, the breeze stills, and the grass seems to shimmer with heat. The lawn, with its running slope, surrounds these two figures with green-gold. May stands close to Edgar, the hem of her blue skirt almost touching his cane. I feel bereft, suddenly, or as if I have become a spirit merely, my flesh melted away; I gaze at my sister and Edgar, and I know I am outside the picture.

In another instant, Edgar calls to Odile, and holds her hand as they walk to the carriage. Mathieu jumps onto the carriage behind me, and Edgar says "Up we go!" and lifts Odile into the air, her pink dress fluttering like a banner.

As he places Odile on the seat, smoothing her dress, he glances at me, and, as quickly as a cat's paw on a meadow, something passes between us, in this bright air. He looks at me as if he knows me, as if he has discovered what I know, and also what I desire.

As we pose, and white clouds sail across the sky and then vanish from my sight, I grow hot in my dress.

"Lyddy!" May's voice startles me.

"Yes?"

"You look half asleep, and Odile too."

"I am sleepy," agrees Odile.

"Can you think of a story to tell, Lyd? I've forgotten the book of fairy tales I meant to bring."

"I can't think of a story, May."

"Then Monsieur Degas will have to think of one."

"*Oui*, Oncle Edgar! Tell them about your journey to Italy, when you were little. Tell them about how you learned to swim, in the stream outside of Naples, and how your brother Achille fell in and almost drowned."

"What a memory you have! Who told you that story?" Degas laughs.

"You did! Just last week!"

"Ah! Well. I think that story must be too sad, or else too boring."

"*Mais non!* It's a good story. You rescued Achille, don't you remember?"

"Ah, yes. Well, either I did, or our tutor. He ended up rather wet, I think, but he was a good type, and we had a splashing fight, while Achille sat on the bank covered in towels, and I defeated my tutor utterly, something he was quite used to, in fact."

"I wish I could swim here," says Odile. "Maybe in the duck pond."

"The duck pond is filthy, *mon chou*. A *gendarme* would fish you out, in any case, and reprimand you severely."

"I would slip away from him, then, and find another place to swim."

"You are a person of exceptional vision and courage, Odile," her uncle says.

viii.

By the time May lets us rest, I am overwhelmed by the heat.

Edgar helps Odile out, and then, with unusual gentleness, he offers me his hand, and I slowly move to the edge of the carriage. He holds my arm as I come down the step.

"You look tired," he says.

"Sit on the blanket, Lyddy," May says, spreading our old picnic blanket with the Scottish plaid on the edge of the lawn. "Mathieu! Go to the café, and buy some camembert and bread. Oh, and see if they have a good pâté, maybe some *saucisson*. We'll have a splendid picnic."

She gives him money. Mathieu looks relieved to stretch, and

then to jump into the driver's seat and flick the whip, touching Bichette's rump.

"Chocolate too, Mathieu!" May calls to him. "And cider!"

"*D'accord, mademoiselle,*" Mathieu shouts, as the carriage rumbles down the *allée,* a cloud of dust blooming behind it.

"I see myself!" says Odile. She's gazing at May's picture. "See my pink dress? And my shoes? I am very, very quiet, aren't I?"

"You are the queen of quietness," says Edgar.

"Mademoiselle Cassatt too," Odile says.

"Mademoiselle Cassatt is astonishingly quiet as well."

Looking at Degas, I am aware of his eyes upon me. He seems to slice through my skin, layer after layer. *So now we know something of each other's secrets,* he seems to say, his eyes dark, inquisitive. *Yes.*

Sitting on the blanket, I can see the picture on May's easel. It has a darkness I had not anticipated. I recognize myself, and Odile, and Mathieu, yet we look odd, somber, as if on a grim errand. Each of us stares in a different direction, but we don't look as if we're really seeing anything. The luscious colors of Odile's face and hair and dress make a splash of brightness, but surrounding her loom darker colors: the black and dusky red of my bonnet, the various blacks of Mathieu's hat and coat, Bichette's tail, the whip. In the background, the trees, which in reality (I glance at them now) look so welcoming and summery, with their crowns of green, appear shadowy. And I look solemn and determined, stoical, as I stare straight ahead, holding the reins and the whip. Of course, the picture is not finished.

I see this painting, suddenly, as a message from May to me. *I know you're on a journey,* the painting says, *to another, darker place. And even though you betray me by leaving, I grant you companions—a child, a groom—to accompany you when I cannot follow. I cannot make your journey joyous, but I promise at least to record your passage.*

May and Edgar sit next to each other, on the other side of the blanket, as Odile comes racing past us, Batty at her heels. When Mathieu returns, he hands the lunch to May, then tosses Batty a stick. May tears the bread, and Edgar opens a pocket knife to cut into the round of cheese. I pour the cider into our glasses.

As I eat the camembert on bread, and taste the delicious little pickles, *cornichons,* I gaze at May's painting. She has pictured something red flowing out of my heart. I look down at my silk jacket and my scarf. They hold different shades of red, yes, but May has changed these reds into something other than a jacket or a scarf, something pouring, a river, with tributaries. And here, around my dress, just under my knees, she's painted a second ribbon of crimson, and on Odile's dress too, bands of another shade, the red of mashed strawberries.

My cider spills in the grass. I right my glass, and rise, moving slowly, as if through water, toward the carriage, hoping to open my parasol. Perhaps this nausea and dizziness come only from the heat.

"Mademoiselle Cassatt! *Vous voyez?* See how Batty can jump!"

I try to smile at Odile as she holds up a stick for Batty, and then the sky, and the trees, and May, and the others, seem to swirl upside down, and I discover that I have collapsed to my knees in the *allée*.

ix.

At home, I am ill again, very ill. I am barely aware who sits next to me in my bedroom. It must be May. I know her touch. I see the deep blue of her dress, but I feel too sick to look at her. She brings me the basin, when I ask her, and she smooths my hair as I open, like a sluice. I am in pain. I am in pain. God help me.

Outside my window, over the sounds of the avenue, I think I hear a child's voice, like the cry of a strange bird, high and floating.

Shadows hover in my room, deep black, gray, even red. I had not thought shadows could come in so many colors.

Lyddy, someone says. It's Mother. Her hand is cool and soft on my forehead. Are you are you all right. I shake my head and I begin to cry. Do you feel pain. Pain. Yes. Shall I call the doctor. What can a doctor do.

Hours pass, days, and I wake to see a girl with taffy-colored hair by my bed. Is this a dream? I wonder, but then I know she is Odile. She wears her hat and a white coat, and gloves. In the shadows stands Edgar. I hope you recover soon, he says to me. Your sister is at a loss without you. I try to smile but my face won't bend that way anymore, and I say, Are you well? And he says, oui, and I ask the child too if she's well, and she says oui, mademoiselle. She holds out a bunch of red tulips, and May takes them, or is it Mother, and says thank you, ma petite, she will love these when she's feeling well enough to gaze at them, and when I look again, Edgar and the child have gone.

I see Thomas, in the afternoon light, sitting calmly at the foot of my bed, gazing at me. You're not dead, then? I ask, bewildered, and he smiles. Well, you see me, don't you? he asks. Yes, I see you. He laughs and shrugs, ordinary and handsome as the day. Bending closer, he asks, Then what is death?

I open my eyes to see May sitting on my bed, dark circles under her eyes. I hold still, waiting for the pain, but for the moment the pain is not here.

"Is it morning?"

"*Oui.*"

"Have I been sick long?"

"*Oui.* Days."

"And—" I hesitate. "Is Odile all right?"

"Of course she is."

"Will she come back?"

"One day, I'm sure. Marguerite decided to take them south, to Nice."

"But the painting?"

"I've finished it."

"How?"

"Well, I painted your face, actually, most of you, before you fell ill, Lyddy, remember? And Mathieu and Odile posed for another couple of days."

"Who held the reins?"

"Louie did. She came with us, to help me finish."

"So—it's done?"

"Yes."

"*Et*—do you like it?"

May looks sad. "I do like it."

"I know it must have come out well, May." *from my heart, a river of red, mute, terrifying*

"Yes. And now you must get better."

But this is a task I seem to have forgotten how to do.

May draws open the curtains, and the light hurts my eyes. How long has it been since I have seen light?

I think of the painting.

And am I on a journey, then? And who goes with me?

xi.

In the afternoon, before May returns, the bell rings, and in a moment I hear Mother talking to someone.

"Degas is here," she says, poking her head into my room. "Would you be able to come say hello?"

The idea of walking from one room to another overwhelms

me, and I feel unnerved, too, at the thought of facing Edgar on my own, without May. I'm not sure why I feel this. I shake my head, and Mother's face disappears.

In a moment, she pokes her head into my room again.

"Could he come in here to see you, Lyddy, just for a moment?"

I hesitate. I must look awful, raggedy and pale; I haven't had a real bath in days.

"I—" I look around my small room, and touch my hand to my hair.

Mother guesses part of my panic. She brushes my hair, sweeping it into a simple *chignon*, and brings me a fresh cap. Then she helps me sit up, and wraps my white shawl around my bed jacket.

When Edgar comes in, Mother gives him the armchair by my bed, and she sits on the ottoman by my dressing table. Looking slightly awkward, beneath his usual ironic pose, he studies my face. For once, to my surprise, I welcome his look. I realize with a stumble of my own heart that I wish to be seen by someone who can see with clarity.

Mother and Edgar chat about his family. When Mother leaves the room for a moment to find her sewing, I look at him. My shyness slips off, like a dress, to the floor around me, something I used to wear.

"You're better?" he asks.

"*Oui, pour le moment.*"

He considers my words.

"A moment can hold great value."

"I wish for more than that."

"Of course you do. Who would not wish for more?"

My eyes sting.

"My family finds it hard to acknowledge how little time I might have. I think May's beginning to acknowledge it."

"*Et toi?* Do you find it hard to acknowledge as well?"

"I don't want to vanish."

"Vanish? *Mais*, the vanishing isn't the point, is it?"

I rub my cheek fiercely. I do not wish to cry. "What's the point then?"

He shrugs. "Seeing. Creating something." He catches my eye now, and holds my gaze. "You do that. You know that, more than most of these types of humanity. You see things, I can tell." *Her arm around his neck, two figures embracing. I claim this picture for my own.* He adds, "You've given more than you may know to your sister."

I have come to a new landscape with this man, a sober place, without many trees. The light shines strongly here, and yet much is in shade. It is not a desert, yet the desire for water, I know, will not be fully satisfied.

"I love her," I say.

"*Oui, évidemment*, and you give her something else, too. You give her—" He pauses, searching for words. "A sense of something terribly valuable, something she must work her way towards, in paint."

"And that's good?"

Edgar laughs a short, sharp laugh. "Good? *Oui, c'est bien*. All of us need something to work towards—to claw our way to, if necessary—to crawl on our bellies to, through mud and across stones, in order to touch and understand a mere part of it."

"But I wish for this myself," I say, astonished at my fierceness. "I wish to be the one clawing, and crawling, surging toward something I love and wish to have."

Naked, this look between us, unhinged. Edgar seems to listen to what I can't say, how I wish to live, to enter the arbor, to swim into the kiss, to break my pose and walk into my own life.

"How do you know you don't?" he asks with quick urgency, his voice low. "How do you know you don't labor towards something? You seem like one who must know about such effort."

"I'm dying."

"*Oui*. I know."

"And I haven't created anything. I have nothing to leave behind me."

"But you allow yourself to be in the picture."

"That's different." My voice sounds harsh, broken.

"Is it? I wonder. And besides, one can labor towards something that never becomes art, or even visible. But you can have it in here." He touches his eyes, and then he bends closer and says, quietly, "You know, you're the one she loves most in the world. She will never love another as well. How can you say you leave nothing behind?" He moves back into his chair, and gazes at me with dark eyes. "You're magnificent, after all."

I let his words float in the air, fall around me, like cherry blossoms. *N'importe quoi*, I would say to anyone else, at any other time, but in this dream-like moment, in this desert, blooming, I accept the words as an unanticipated gift.

Degas rubs his eyes, and I think of something May told me a couple of weeks ago.

"His eyes are bad."

"Bad?"

"He can't see well. When he looks at something, he can't see the center."

"How can that be? He paints. He paints constantly."

May looks at me soberly and shrugs. "Of course he paints."

"But—what will happen?"

"I don't know. He thinks he may go blind."

Lydia Seated at an Embroidery Frame

and then I'm holding a small May's hand, and we're in the meadow behind our house at Hardwicke, and we walk through the high grass, among the fireflies, through the gate and past the barn, and the garden, toward the house, and I can see light inside, and Ella's at the front door, waving us in for bed, and

i.

Sewing the piece of silk onto my embroidery frame after breakfast, I picture Elsie's clear eyes.

"What do you think Elsie would like on her pillowcase?" I call to Mother, who's reading the paper in her bedroom.

Mother comes slowly to my door. I hear her slippered steps on the rug, her sighs.

"Have you looked in those, Lyddy?" She motions toward my pattern-box and the magazines piled on my dressing table.

"I've looked through everything."

"You might try flowers again." Mother plumps herself on my bed and takes off her specs, cleaning them with her shawl.

"Elsie's can't look too much like Sister's, though." For Sister, I embroidered a pillowcase with a border of roses, twining, *like the roses in the arbor, one hot day in August, scorching, fragrant.*

"What about wildflowers?"

"Wildflowers. Yes." Perfect, I think, for isn't Elsie just like a wildflower, brightly colored and uncultivated? I wish children could always stay that way. May is more like that, still, than most women I've ever known. I remember, last summer, how Elsie couldn't restrain herself from picking the flowers in the garden. May and I took her to the riverbank and let her gather bunches of wildflowers, instead, and grass too, which seemed to Elsie as splendid as flowers.

"I know American wildflowers best, though," I say.

"Well, Elsie's an American, through and through," Mother says drily. "I still have my book of American wildflowers." She pushes herself off the bed, and walks slowly out of my room. "I'll find it for you."

As I pore over the pictures in her book, I relish the flowers' names, the way they seem to sing and to bite: trillium, columbine, dogtooth violet. I yearn suddenly for my sketchbook, the one in which I drew wildflowers in pen and watercolor the summer I agreed to marry Thomas. I wonder if Mother still has it, stowed away in a chest, here or in America, or if it sits somewhere among Aleck's papers.

I mark the wildflowers I like best, and then I begin to sketch a design on paper. I want something modern, not old-fashioned—a clean, spare form. I toss out design after design. I'll know the right one when it comes to me.

Our apartment feels quiet today. Father has gone riding, and Mother is reading now in her room. May is at her studio, I think (*and who is with her? and what do they do? I picture Edgar lounging on the chair near her, smoking, rubbing his eyes, the pigeons whirring, May talking to her new model*).

Today I feel as if I have fallen out of the whole picture. Sometimes, this morning, I have the sense of foreknowledge: *this is how the world will be when you are no longer here. This is how it will go on without you.* I wish to throw my arms around the day, embrace it fiercely, make it impossible for it to let me go.

That afternoon, a month ago, when Edgar Degas came to my bedside, he seemed to offer me a picture of myself, one to strive towards. In this picture, I possessed grace and strength and valor. And he had the kindness to claim that it was I who had presented him with such a vision. *"You show me how to live,"* he said, *"if only I could do it as you do."*

One June afternoon, I begin my stitching on Elsie's silk. I try to pour all my thoughts into this one task, this here and now. I've been so ill this month that I'm beginning to wonder whether I'll ever pose for May again, or whether she'll even ask me.

I've designed seven circles, to be stitched in a grass-green running stitch, on the white ground, each one framing a wildflower. I've chosen flowers I hope Elsie will recognize: buttercups, Indian paintbrush, wild sweet William, clover, pink lady's slippers, bee balm, wild columbine.

I hear May open the front door. She comes into my room as I'm threading the needle with a yellow silk, to begin the buttercups. She looks as if she's run up the five flights of stairs to our apartment.

"You're home early."

"Yes, I am."

May pulls off her burgundy gloves and lays them over the wooden bar of my embroidery frame. She looks hot.

"Did you go to the gallery?"

"Yes. I saw some good things there. I'll have to bring Louie back with me and urge her to buy something. Renoir has a new one for sale, and Camille Pissarro has some good things."

"*Et* Degas?"

May touches my embroidery frame. "Degas has a stunning pastel. I should buy it, just so you can see it. I'm thinking of urging Louie to buy it."

She looks over my shoulder.

"Oh, Lyddy, I like your design."

I hear a new note in May's voice: sorrow, is it? or just tiredness? She walks about my room, touching my hairbrush, smoothing my bed, straightening my books.

"You're reading Tennyson?" she asks, opening a little gold book.

"Yes."

"Ah! 'The Lotos-Eaters.'"

She sits in the armchair by my bed and begins to read.

After a while I ask, "What are you painting these days, May?"

She looks up and shrugs. "Oh, not much. I started another picture, with a friend of Louie's as a model, but it didn't go well."

"Are you sure?"

"It was all right, just—a bit flat. I'm looking for a new idea, really."

"And your prints?"

"I'm tired of prints, for the moment."

May reads, as I stitch one of my buttercups.

"Lyddy."

I look up.

"Could I paint you again?"

Her question almost makes me tremble, I'm not sure why.

"I look dreadful."

"How can you say that? You look just like yourself."

"I have no color."

"You're simply fair." May gives me a teasing smile. "I'll give you color, *de toute manière*."

"I feel so heavy, May, you've no idea. I'm like a hippopotamus in my slowness, these days. I'm not sure I could even walk as far as your studio. I have such stupid aches."

"I can paint you right here, then."

"*Ici?*"

"In your room."

"*Mais*—the oil paints will smell, won't they? And there's hardly space enough." I look around my room.

"The smell won't be so bad. We'll air it out each day, afterward. And I can manage with the space."

I look at her face, the shadows under her eyes.

"Do you have no other model right now, May?"

"Of course I have other models. It's you I want. I've been dreaming about this picture, Lyddy, of you at your embroidery."

You allow yourself to be in the picture. A sense of something terribly valuable.

"All right. I will."

"Merci." May embraces me hard. "Do you think you could begin tomorrow morning?"

"Tomorrow morning, yes."

May rises and opens my wardrobe. She sifts through my dresses.

"And—could you wear this dress?" She holds up my salmon-pink silk with the high collar and the flower-print.

"Bien sûr, of course I will."

iii.

In the morning, after breakfast, I put on my salmon-pink dress, and arrange my hair, and then I look at the buttercups I stitched yesterday. I can picture Elsie tracing the green stems and the buttery flowers, with her finger, before she sleeps on a hot summer's night, when the light still holds on the lawn outside her window, or on a night in the middle of winter, when all the world seems hoary and blank, and her pillow is a field.

Remember me, I wish to say to this young niece. *Don't allow me to be forgotten.* And isn't this what I wish to say to May, and to others? To

Edgar too, the one I had always thought of as merely brutal, whose kindness shimmers, in a certain light, like quick gold brushstrokes touching his shoulders, his face, throwing one utterly off guard. *You're magnificent, he said, and I thought in that instant, to my great surprise, if I could love anyone now, it would be this man, arrogant and imperfect as he is, for in that moment, in our strange landscape, I felt shaken, touched, as if he had opened up my very flesh. I know this is not love as May knows it, but it is a kind of love, springing from some hard truth, gazed at together, truth and longing.*

When May comes in with her easel, I notice her burgundy gloves, still draped over the frame.

"Shouldn't you move your gloves, May?"

May follows my glance to the frame.

"I had forgotten the gloves, but actually, I like them there, Lyd. I think they add something."

I shrug. As May sets up her easel, and prepares to paint, I thread my needle with a light blue floss, for the wild sweet William, and begin a fishbone stitch for the petals. Each small flower has five petals, like five slender blue hearts, and all of these flowers together create a burst of color.

I almost hold my breath as I try the first few stitches. I can never be sure if my design will come out right. The color shines against the white ground, and in a few minutes I can see that the petals, although simple, will look much like the myriad petals of a sweet William.

iv.

"Could you hold your hands still for a moment, Lyddy?"

I hold still, gazing at my right hand, held just above the silk, in the act of pushing the needle through. The needle shines, silvery, in my fingers. Mother's porcelain thimble crowns my second finger. The silk is pierced by silver. I keep my left hand still, just under the cloth, holding the needle as it comes through beneath.

May sits so close to me that I can hear the smallest rustle of her skirt. Her lemony cologne mingles with the stronger smell of the oils.

When Edgar visits, in the late morning, he looks hot and winded. As I break my pose, I can see his damp shirt beneath his summer coat. I feel a kind of humming inside me.

"Your sister told me you were posing for her again," he says. "I wished to see for myself."

I smile, and my face grows hot. *And are you in love, then?* I ask myself. *And what do you expect to happen? Nothing. Nothing. Only this, his eyes upon me, the air between us quickly threaded through with something blue, gold, barely visible. I can have this much.*

May is looking at me, curious. She looks as if she's forgotten what she's doing, why she's here. She almost asks me something, but then seems to think better of it.

All I can think is that this humming is something I acknowledge and accept. I am guilty of nothing more.

Degas tosses himself into the chair by my bed, as May helps me find my pose again. She touches my shoulder—"Good, Lyd"—and then my chin—"*C'est bien.*" Before she moves away, she holds her hand to my cheek. Her hand is warm, and I am for a dazed moment on a lawn in Pennsylvania with May, *her small hand hot on my cheek, as she turns my face toward her to gain my attention. Lyddy.*

I feel my face hot, still, as I look at my embroidery, the needle threaded with a rich purple for the wild columbine. I make a few stitches with the floss, hoping I can fill in one part of this upside-down flower, this gay plumage, fool's cap, before May asks me to hold my pose.

"Would you like me to read?" Edgar asks. "How about this? Tennyson?"

Lydia at a Tapestry Frame, Collection of the Flint Institute of Arts, Gift of the Whiting Foundation, 1967.32.

I know May will ask for "The Lady of Shalott," and she does. It was her favorite when she was little. Tennyson's words, in Degas' voice and accent, seem to break off bits of color, the rhymes sweeping the colors into arcs, as strong as nets.

She left the web, she left the loom,
She made three paces through the room,
She saw the water-lily bloom,
She looked down to Camelot.

I used to love this poem, although I find it a bit sillier now, too romantic and melodramatic, and Edgar seems to think so too, for he adds a touch of mockery to his reading, undercutting Tennyson's sense of tragedy, as the Lady sings her dying song, on her way to Camelot, heartsick for love of Lancelot. Yet, as Edgar reaches the end, his voice becomes more serious. May and I join him for the last lines, from memory.

He said, 'She has a lovely face;
God in his mercy lend her grace,
The Lady of Shalott.'

The poem floats in the room.

"*Pas mal*," Edgar says. I look at my fingers, pushing the needle through, with the deep purple thread. I wish I could see his face. I feel his eyes on me, scraping and gentle, grave and amused, passionate and objective.

"You must wish for a rest, Lyddy?" May asks.

"I'm all right," I say, but I think, *No, it's not rest I desire, but to be here, with this light, this needle, these eyes.*

vii.

After tea, May dresses, to see friends, she says, at the Comédie Française. I picture Edgar, sitting just behind her, half in shadow.

After writing a letter to each of Aleck's children, I stand in the lamplight, in my bare feet and robe, looking at the painting May has begun of me. It's already a striking picture, showing a woman behind an embroidery frame, sewing, her head bent forward. A waterfall of white splashes on the left side of the canvas—the curtain, that must be. May has made a line, in gold, along my neck and shoulder, and my right arm. She has brought the most detail to my face so far. But what is that splash of deep burgundy, almost black, near the middle of the picture? Looking at my embroidery frame, I see May's new gloves lying peacefully over the top.

a sense of something terribly valuable

In bed, I open my Tennyson to "Tithonus." A luscious, slow-moving poem, a love-poem of sorts.

I wither slowly in thine arms, / Here at the quiet limit of the world.

I wake out of a dream (*I am on a boat, and the sky has grown dark. Someone stands behind me, touching my arm. As I turn, I see that it is Edgar, only he's younger, much younger, his face more open, eager. He brings my hand halfway to his mouth, and*). A figure shadows my doorway. I am frightened for a moment (*a woman was murdered just last week in Paris, I remember, the details lurid in the papers*), but of course the figure is simply May. Her white nightgown glimmers in the blacks and grays of my room. She eases herself around the embroidery frame, where the white silk floats like a dusky window.

"Lyddy."

"Yes, May."

"May I come into your bed?"

May has not made such a request in a dozen years at least—

more—although when she was little she often slept in my bed; I knew, whenever we moved to a new house, she would come down the dark hallway and slip into my bed for reassurance, night after night. We moved so often.

I raise the duvet, and May comes in beside me. I give her part of my pillow and touch her face. Wet, is it? I stroke her cheek, and she comes close, her arms around me, her face cradled in the hollow between my shoulder and my breast.

"Are you all right, May?"

I touch her hair. My dream lingers strangely.

Wrapping my arms about her, I feel her delicate shoulder blades, her thin arms. She smells like tobacco smoke, bittersweet, and wine, and something else too, licorice maybe, or sweet, ripe pears. Her lemon cologne is faint now. She seems hot, almost feverish. Her hair brushes against my neck.

"Was the play good, May?"

"*Oui.*"

May moves away from me. She sits on my bed in the dark now, close to me. I can almost see her hair, thick and curling around her shoulders. I cannot see her face.

"I went to Edgar's house afterwards," she adds after a moment. I'm surprised, and can't at first think what to say.

"*Ah bon!* Who went with you?"

"Oh, a few people," May says carefully. "I don't think you know them."

"Did you enjoy their company?"

her arm around his neck, her face joyous

She lies next to me again, on her back. I can see her face gleaming pale in the dark. She's quiet for a long time, and then she says slowly, "Yes. Yes, I did."

I urge myself to be glad for my sister, to grant her her invisible triumph, known only to herself, and, in all quietness, to me. *Good jumping, May, Aleck says, and I say, Be careful.*

May's voice swims out of the dark, thick and strangely harsh. "You won't leave me, will you, Lyddy?"

May brings her face to my shoulder. I feel the heat of her breath on my skin.

"Stay here, don't be sick. I won't be able to live if you become really sick again, and leave me."

"You will, though, May. *Tu vivras.* You'll live as well as you possibly can."

I'm overwhelmed by him.

"I won't be able to paint."

"You will paint. You'll paint gorgeous things."

153

I'll come and see what you do.

"You don't understand, Lyddy. You can't know. I need to know you're in the world. No one else is like you. *Personne.*" She adds, "I always thought I'd have you."

You're the one she loves most in the world.

Then what is death?

"Well, you have me still. *Je suis encore là.*"

I lie awake in the darkness and listen as May's breathing becomes more regular. I hear the city's early-morning sounds: horses on pavement, someone calling to another, a train in the distance. I hold my sister, against the darkness.

viii.

The sky glitters this morning, almost turquoise. Paris shimmers, laid out in a bowl of gay shapes. How strange to be ill on such a day.

Sitting at my embroidery frame after breakfast, posing for May, I gaze again at my wild columbine. I've been able to make only a few stitches. I yearn to fill in my second flower. My back aches, and I cannot feel the thimble on my second finger. I cannot even feel the needle, either above or below the silk ground.

I was sick again this morning, and May looked discouraged as she helped me wash my face and get dressed. I wonder whether this will be May's last picture of me. I think May wonders this too, because there's a new quietness between us. She's intensely focused on her work, and she paints for a long time without a pause.

When Mother comes in for a little while, to read to us, I ask her for "Tithonus," because this poem hovers in my mind today. As she approaches the end, I listen to each word.

> *Yet hold me not for ever in thine East:*
> *How can my nature longer mix with thine?*
> *Coldly thy rosy shadows bathe me, cold*
> *Are all thy lights, and cold my wrinkled feet*
> *Upon thy glimmering thresholds*

"Is Degas coming for tea this week, May?" Mother asks, after she's finished reading.

"Yes, I think so."

> *Release me, and restore me to the ground*

"Is he busy these days?"

"*Oui.* Very."

Thou seest all things, thou wilt see my grave:
Thou wilt renew thy beauty morn by morn.

"Do you think you'll put this one in the Impressionist exhibition, next year?"

"*Je l'espère.*"

Thou wilt renew thy beauty morn by morn;
I earth in earth forget these empty courts,
And thee returning on thy silver wheels.

X.

Two more days of posing, and on the third day, after a long morning, May says, "Time to rest, Lyddy." Her voice sounds oddly gentle. As I move out of my pose, I see May absorbed in putting away her paints.

"The light's changed, Lyddy. We should stop."

May looks at me for a moment, her hand on her hip.

"Would you like to see? I think I almost have it."

I can't imagine May painting another, at least of me, that I could love as well.

In the picture, I bend slightly toward my embroidery, utterly absorbed in what I'm sewing. One can see the silk ground only from underneath, where my hand dissolves into loose brush-strokes, deep pink, white, blue-gray. *What are you embroidering,* I ask myself, *a landscape? a boat?* It could be anything. I'm bent at my labor.

I see now that May's painting creates a kind of memory. Whether or not anyone ever knew me, she will offer a memory of me, for the world to claim. And I see something else: she pictures me as a woman who has had her wishes fulfilled. The day is luminous, the woman's dress a meadow, as she bends to her creation, on her own, desirous simply of what she already has. I yearn to be like this, to have the grace of such satisfaction.

"You've made a whole world, May."

"You like the feeling of it?"

"It's very absorbing."

"I like the way this turned out." May points to the line of the embroidery frame, and I follow her finger right up to the maroon splotch in the middle—her gloves. I think, surely May will be doing more with that. Surely she won't leave it here, marring such a perfect image.

But May says, "I could almost call it done right now."

"Are you sure?"

"*Oui.*"

I gaze at the daubs of paint, especially in the lower half of the painting. Suddenly the whole picture seems to waver. To allow that paint to stay, so unformed—has she ever done this so fully?

"Will you do more with her hand?"

"Maybe not. I like it like that. It's like photographs, Lyddy, when the person moves, or the camera moves, and things blur."

"Yes, I can see that. But in a painting, you have a chance to catch things very still?" I think of the hours I've sat here, my neck aching, precisely to help her paint such stillness.

"But what if things aren't always meant to stay still, Lyddy? Think of it. The world moves, the light changes. Your hand moves, as you embroider."

"But it wasn't moving all the time."

"But if I hadn't been painting you, and you'd simply been embroidering, it would have been."

I feel confused, as if I'm trying to present an important argument to May, but I've lost the thread. *Why not allow incompleteness, change?* I think, and I almost laugh, as I realize how May has met my own thoughts. Even this image of utter satisfaction must show its own artifice, its fragility, its readiness to dissolve into paint, the raggedness of desire.

If May has painted me on an island, then, she has made clear how the sand shifts, how the water works at it, shapes it, dissolves it. When there's lightning, a tree falls, and lizards dart into the underbrush. *And that river of color, there* (I study the maroon, the burgundy—what color is it?): *maybe that's the mud of the island itself, or the blood* (my blood), *the unformed stuff of it. And is it the blood of illness, then, or of life? Or is it of illness and life, both, all rolled together in a terrifying and luscious stream?* It's over my heart, in the picture, almost as if it springs from my heart, or from May's toward me. She knows more about me than I had thought. The color is at once a mistake and a defiant splash: *Here I am, pigment, stuff, the raw material, and what are you going to do about it? It's blood, and desire, and love, and pain, and fury. You can't staunch it. The question is: how to live with it?*

xi.

After lunch, May comes to the threshold of my room, where I am threading a lavender floss to begin Elsie's clover. She buttons her summer coat.

"You're going out?" I ask.

"Yes."

She comes in, and quietly takes her burgundy gloves from my embroidery frame.

"To your studio?"

"To a gallery, first, and then to my studio."

I look at her, and she returns my look with her own, teasing, profound.

When she kisses me, I smell her cologne, her freshly washed hair. I catch a glimpse, under her fur collar, of a necklace I have not seen before—pearl, with tiny rubies.

"*Merci*, Lyddy."

"What have I done?"

"You've posed. You've helped me paint." She adds, "I hope you'll be able to pose again soon."

"I hope so too," I say.

Here is what I write. I write it as a letter to May, but I do not wish her to see it, not yet. I put it into my pattern box.

My sister, my soul—when I dissolve, in my heart's blood, I know you will think that you will dissolve too. Your heart will be sore; it will scatter into brush-strokes, fragments, feathers, and you will think you too will vanish. But here is what I wish to tell you. Listen well, May. You will remember me, then, bent over my labor, at my embroidery frame, on a hot June day in Paris, my dress like a field of flowers, my face calm. You will remember me, because you caught my soul in paint. And one day you'll pick up your brush again, and stretch a new canvas, you'll bend to your work again, and the world at your elbow, or crying from the newspapers, or whispering in the shadows near you, will become quieter for a moment, and you will put all these things aside, to make again a world to stand next to that other world, the one we think we know, and you'll hear me whispering, Courage, May, and you'll bend to it, again and again.

Je t'embrasse,

Lyddy

Writing this, I feel almost happy. Sometimes one can have a glimpse of the future, and, frightening as it is, it can have in it an element of consolation. Terrible, to imagine a world continuing beyond my own dissolving; yet what if I am a presence for May, and for others too, leaving a trace, like the swath of white light on the top of this embroidery frame? Maybe I should not be so afraid of vanishing, after all.

In the morning, after May has left, I walk into my room to look at Elsie's pillowcase, stretched out still, on my frame, with my designs, yellow, blue, green, purple, lavender. This too is a letter. Poignant but sturdy, this desire to touch another, to reach across an ocean, or a city, or a room. (*Tell me how to live as you do, he said, with such grace. I know nothing about grace.*) My wildflowers look most imperfect. But, slowly, I thread my needle, with a red for the Indian paintbrush, and I begin to sew. Soon, I will create the bee balm too, and then I'll be ready to cut the threads and send this silk field sailing.

I yearn to be simply present in this day, filled for the moment with color and shape, my own hand urging the needle through the silk.

Lydia Cassatt became very ill in the summer of 1881.

She died in Paris on November 7, 1882, of Bright's Disease.

Mary Cassatt painted and created prints for over thirty more years.

She died at her château in Beaufresne, in 1926.

I am indebted, in this work of fiction, to the superb scholarship on Mary Cassatt and the Impressionists. I am especially indebted to the work of George Hersey, Anne Higonnet, and Nancy Mowll Mathews. The recent exhibition of Cassatt's oeuvre, organized by Judith A. Barter, and the rich accompanying catalogue, *Mary Cassatt: Modern Woman*, have contributed to my understanding of Cassatt's art, family life, and relationship to the world of late nineteenth-century French culture. I wish to thank my research assistant, Jennifer Boittin, for her valuable help.